# Cords
# of Love

*Lynn A. Coleman*

Heartsong Presents

To my granddaughter, Leanna Marie, who was going through the "why" stage when I was writing this story. I love you and pray God's continued blessing on you.

**A note from the author:**
*I love to hear from my readers! You may correspond with me by writing:*

> Lynn A. Coleman
> Author Relations
> PO Box 719
> Uhrichsville, OH 44683

ISBN 1-58660-620-4

**CORDS OF LOVE**

All scripture quotations, unless otherwise indicated, are taken from the HOLY BIBLE, NEW INTERNATIONAL VERSION ®. NIV®. Copyright © 1973, 1978, 1984 by International Bible Society. Used by permission of Zondervan Publishing House. All rights reserved.

All of the characters and events in this book are fictitious. Any resemblance to actual persons, living or dead, or to actual events is purely coincidental.

*Cover illustration @ Getty One, Inc..*

PRINTED IN THE U.S.A.

## one

The bell above the door jingled. Renee looked up. "Aaron, how'd the appointment go?"

"Not good. They went with the competition." Aaron Chapin, her boss, rubbed the back of his neck.

"What?" Renee stood up. That was impossible. They'd worked hard on that proposal. "What happened?"

Renee sent a quick glance to John, an art major at a local college who did part-time work for Sunny Flo Designs. He bit his lower lip and looked back at his drafting table.

Aaron's gaze locked with hers, his dark brown eyes appearing almost black. "They said we weren't original," he answered, his words tight.

"They're crazy. No one, absolutely no one, has anything on the Web marginally like that. I checked." Renee tapped the top of her desk with her recently manicured fingernails.

"Apparently, that's not the case. The competition gave them something very similar at a fraction of the price." In a couple of brisk strides, Aaron sequestered himself in the back room of the store, where he kept a couple chairs, coffee table, refrigerator, coffee machine, and a love seat. He often used the room to go over proposals with customers.

A desire to comfort him washed over her. The poor man had seen more than his share of suffering. His wife had died in an auto accident two years before. Her heart went out to him, a single parent raising a four-year-old son, Adam, who happened to be the cutest little guy she'd ever seen.

She squeezed her eyes closed and covered them with her thumb and forefinger. *Why'd he have to be so vulnerable, Lord?* she silently prayed. *What if I become attracted to him?*

She'd keep her distance. Renee sat down at her desk,

5

glanced at the computer monitor, then retyped the advertising slogan she'd been working on all morning.

"Psst," John whispered. "I'm bailing before Aaron asks me to put in overtime tonight. Midterms are staring me in the face. I haven't even cracked the book open from my civics class."

"No problem. I'll stay if he has a mind to work."

John reached for his blue backpack, swung it over his shoulder, and hustled out the door. "Tell Aaron I'll be in after class tomorrow."

Renee waved him off and turned back to her computer screen. The I-beam blinked at her, beckoning some new words of inspiration. She snuck a peek back toward the open door to the back room. No sound. Nothing. Should she check on him? *No,* she reminded herself. *I've already decided not to pry.*

She tapped the keys of the keyboard. "Office relationships never work out," she mumbled.

&

Aaron stirred his coffee. How on earth could he have lost this account? They'd come up with a unique angle and twist to the Web design. Something not yet on the Web. He dropped the wooden coffee stirrer into the trash.

The phone rang.

"Sunny Flo Designs, Renee speaking. May I help you?"

Renee Austin had been a gold mine. The woman knew Web design and graphic layout, and she added the creative edge he felt he'd been losing. But how long could he afford to keep her on if he kept losing accounts like this one? *Stop it,* he reprimanded himself. *It's only one account; it's not the world. There will be more accounts, Sunny Flo is—*

"Aaron, Adam's on line one," Renee called out.

He picked up the receiver and sat down on the soft white leather love seat. Hannah had picked out the set; it worked well with the laid-back yet professional atmosphere. "Hey, Buddy, what's up?"

"Dad, Grandma said I had to call you about supper."

"Oh." Which meant Adam had been giving his grandmother

a hard time about what he wanted to eat. "Tell Grandma I'll be picking you up for supper."

"Really?" The joy in his son's voice tugged at his heart.

"Really. My appointment canceled."

"Yipee!" Adam screamed as Aaron pulled the phone from his ear.

"I'll see you in a little while, Sport."

"Okay. Bye, Dad."

"Bye, Son." He clicked the portable phone off.

Of all the days to have an account fall through. Perhaps it had been his fault. He never should have scheduled such an important client the day before. . .

Yes, he'd lost the account, pure and simple. His mind hadn't been on his work. "God, why?" He rubbed his face as tears threatened his eyes. *Not at work.*

He picked up a tissue and blew his nose, then stormed into the bathroom and splashed his face with cold water and patted it dry. He heard the phone ring again. Aaron listened, thankful Renee hadn't called him. He sat down for a moment with the light off. His mind drifted back to the accident. Shaking, he recalled the vision of Hannah's mangled car, the blood—so much blood. "Oh, God, please take these memories away. I. . . When won't I have to deal with them anymore?"

Who was he kidding? He knew those images would be with him the rest of his life. He'd been told not to go see the vehicle. He'd been told to get a close family friend to go, but he hadn't listened. He'd always been stubborn. Aaron didn't know if he'd gotten that from his prideful Yankee father or the hot-tempered blood of his Cuban mother. Often he figured it came from both of them, making him an immovable object on far too many occasions. And because of that streak, he'd been left with nightmarish images. Currently those images tore at his soul, tore at the fabric of his beliefs. No man should see how his wife suffered before her death, especially following the impact of a tractor-trailer careening into a small SUV.

His eyes fully adjusted to the darkness of the small rest room as the meager light revealed the mirror and sink, the toilet paper roll that needed to be replaced soon, and the framed picture of his first layout ad. He'd been fresh out of college and on top of the world then. Hannah had saved it, and when he'd branched out to start his own business, she'd had it framed and then presented it to him the day Sunny Flo Designs opened.

"Enough." He stood and washed his face with cold water once again. *It's been two years. Get used to it,* he resolved. Stepping back into the conference area, he picked up the phone and called his mother. "Hi, Mom. Did Adam tell you?"

*"Si,* when will you be arriving?"

Aaron turned his wrist and glanced at the metal hands that displayed the time. "I figure in an hour."

"All right, Son. I'll have him ready. Unless you'd like to stay for dinner?"

He'd love to. His cooking skills were vastly inferior. But he didn't want to leave himself vulnerable with his family. "Thanks, but no. I think I'll take him to his favorite restaurant."

"The cheese place?"

"Uh-huh."

His mother groaned. He couldn't blame her. The place was for children, and they ran wild from one game to another. The food was for kids too—pizza, hot dogs, hamburgers—and the noise of the place sent more than one parent home with a headache. Grandparents seemed particularly susceptible.

After a quick good-bye, he went to his desk.

"Aaron, John has a layout on his drafting table you'll want to look at." Renee walked over toward John's work area.

Why'd he have to hire a woman, a blond-haired, blue-eyed temptation? He should have known better and overlooked her superior work compared to the other applicants.

"Thank you. How's the work on this year's tennis championship coming?"

Renee stepped back to her desk. "Take a look. I've just about worked out the kinks with the Java script. The tennis ball isn't too busy, and I like the speed at which it comes across on my screen. But we need to check it out on the older computer and see how it performs."

Renee thought Aaron wise to keep an old computer with a dial-up modem off-line to check out the Web pages they were creating. They'd upload them in a secured location on the company's Web site and view them on-line. They'd circumvented quite a few problems that way. Not everyone had the latest and greatest software on their personal computers.

She glanced over to Aaron. His face seemed puffy, his back stiffer than usual. The tension he'd been carrying for the past week seemed to be growing.

*It's none of your business; just keep your mind to yourself. You don't need to be messing with this man's troubles. Didn't you have enough problems before?* The sting of Brent's horrible actions came back into focus. How could he have done such a thing?

"Renee, look at scores.htm."

Renee clicked on the button. What was he seeing? "I'm there."

"Scroll down halfway."

"I'm there." She scanned the document. "What's that?" she yelped. *Where'd that purple line come from?*

Aaron chuckled. "That was my question to you."

Renee looked over the code. Sure enough, it was in there, but how? She hadn't put it in, had she? What was she working in purple for? "That's really strange. I don't recall doing this."

"Probably a copy and paste without realizing it."

Renee quickly fixed the glitch.

The phone rang. Aaron picked it up. "Sunny Flo Designs."

"Hi, Mom." He paused, then added, "Sure, you can drop him off."

He leaned forward in his chair. "What? Is she all right?"

Renee watched him clench his fist, then swivel the back of his chair to her. Right, it was none of her business. Then why did she care so much?

Aaron's mumbled words ended with the click of the handset in its cradle.

"I'll be right back." He stormed out the door and marched across the parking lot to the small café.

Renee shrugged her shoulders and looked back at the screen. Aaron Chapin didn't need her messing up on any further accounts.

"Hey, Renee, how's it going?" John walked back through the doors.

"Fine. I thought you were studying for midterms."

John came over and looked past her to her computer screen. "I forgot my textbook. Where's the boss?"

"Next door; he's on edge." She highlighted the foreign coding and hit the delete key.

"Well, it is that time of year." John's thin frame, wild curls, and baggy jeans reminded her of her own college days.

"What time of year?"

John straddled his stool like a cowboy on a horse and thumbed through the piles on his desk for the book. "Anniversary of his wife's death. It was sometime this month. I wager by the way he's been acting, it's this week or next."

*And to have lost the account too—no wonder he retreated into seclusion.* "Guess we better just mind ourselves and keep busy."

"Nope, I'm outta here." John jumped up and slipped out the front door as fast as he'd entered.

"Does he go off the deep end, Lord?" Renee looked for her purse. Perhaps she should call it a day too. She opened her desk drawer to retrieve her wallet.

"Where'd John go?" Aaron asked as he came back in.

"Uh, he said he'd be back tomorrow."

"Great." Aaron's temper was beginning to show.

"Aaron," she whispered.

He turned toward her and came up beside her. His finely bronzed skin, dark eyes, and dark hair seemed imposing. She'd hate to anger the man.

"Are you all right?" she asked tentatively.

"I'm fine." The edge on his words could have cut steel.

Instantly a look of regret crossed his face. "Sorry. Look, I know you're a Christian and, well, I'd like you to pray for someone. She's just been beaten by her husband and has landed in the hospital."

"Oh my. I'll definitely pray. What's her name, if you don't mind me asking?"

"Marie." His hands shook. "She's my sister."

Her sympathy for this man took control. She eased out of her chair and walked around her desk. "I'm sorry, Aaron. I'll pray."

He nodded and started to retreat toward the back room.

Renee hesitated. Should she follow? Should she show compassion? Did he want it? She wouldn't be much of a Christian if she didn't reach out to him. Cautiously, she entered the back room.

He sat on the chair angled to the right of the love seat.

She sat down in front of him on the coffee table. "Aaron, John said your wife died around this time of year."

He raised his head and narrowed his gaze upon hers. "Yes," he croaked out.

"I'm sorry. Can I do anything for you?" She cupped his hand with her own.

His gaze changed. He reached out and touched her hair. She didn't move—she couldn't move.

"It's so silky," he whispered.

Odd, he'd been married; he knew what a woman's hair felt like. Then she remembered that his wife was Spanish. Perhaps she had more of the South American Indian's style of hair.

He slowly rubbed the ends of her hair with his thumb and forefinger. "Hannah's was soft, but in a different way," he mumbled. "I miss her, Renee. I really, really miss her. Why did God allow her to die?"

What could she say? She didn't know? She'd never understood her own losses. Her parents had died when she was only eight. She'd been sent to live with her aunt, who gave her a roof over her head but was too caught up with her male friends to take much notice of her niece.

His thumb touched her cheek.

Renee closed her eyes and swallowed hard.

He pulled her toward him, then his soft lips blazed against her own. She pulled back and reached up to slap his face but caught the shock in his eyes.

"I'm sorry. I don't know what came over me. It'll never happen again." Aaron jumped up and rushed out of the room.

"Daddy!" Adam called as the front door banged behind him.

## two

"Hey, Buddy." Aaron scooped up his son and held him close. What had come over him? He didn't want to know. He didn't want to explore it. He didn't even want to think about it.

Noticing his mother waving from her car at the curb, Aaron returned the gesture as she drove off. And what about Marie? What could he do for her? Manuel needed to go to prison for his actions. He was a drunk and abusive. As much as Aaron wanted to go to his sister's side, he had an errand to do.

The café sent over two brown bags full of the meals he'd ordered. "Miss Austin," Aaron called, "I'm leaving now. Would you lock up?"

"Sure," she squeaked out from the back room. She hadn't come out. He couldn't blame her. He wouldn't be surprised to find her resignation on his desk in the morning.

Aaron didn't want to face her; he couldn't. He put Adam down and gave him one of the bags to carry. "Here ya go, Son. We'll bring these down to your cousins."

He'd ordered enough food for his sister's four kids, Adam, and himself. He'd take them to a park to eat. He had no idea what condition the house was in or if Manuel would be there. In one warped part of Aaron's brain, he hoped he could show Manuel what it was like to be beaten to a pulp. Not that the man would feel it in a drunken stupor.

"Daddy, is *Tia* Marie okay?"

Sweat beaded between Aaron's shoulders as they crossed the parking lot to his van. Aaron secured Adam in the booster seat. "She'll be all right, Son. She's been hurt."

"I know. Uncle Manuel beat her."

"Who told you?"

The boy looked down at his sneaker-covered toes. "No one.

I heard Grandma telling you in Spanish."

"You understood those words?"

Adam nodded his head.

Aaron grinned and mussed the boy's hair. "You're too smart."

"Momma spoke in Spanish, and Grandma speaks in Spanish all the time. Grandpa does a little."

Aaron hadn't been teaching Adam Spanish, hadn't thought about it one way or the other. He knew Adam knew some phrases, but apparently he'd picked up far more.

"Is your dog red and your nose green?" Aaron asked him in Spanish.

He wiggled and giggled. "Daddy, we don't have a dog."

Aaron slipped behind the steering wheel. "No, we don't. Can you answer me in Spanish?"

"No. I understand it, but I don't say the words so good."

"We'll work on it together, okay?"

*"Si."* Adam grinned.

The entire trip to his sister's place in Homestead, south of Miami, they practiced Spanish. Adam had a natural ear for the language. He'd grown up with it. They practiced silly sentences that worked on rolling the *R*s, which became more and more difficult as silliness worked into the conversation.

On their arrival, they found Aaron's nephews and nieces at the neighbors and no sign of Manuel. Reluctantly, the children piled into the van. He took them to a park and made a picnic out of the meal he'd brought with them.

Aaron tapped out his father's cell phone number. "Hey, Dad, how is she?"

"She's going to be all right. He broke her arm this time."

Aaron kicked a hunk of coral. "He needs to be arrested," he mumbled into the phone and prayed the kids didn't hear him.

"Yes, but your sister is too afraid of him once he's released."

"It's not right." Aaron knew his father felt the same way, but until Marie was ready to remove herself from the situation, their hands were tied. In the past they'd tried to file police reports, only to have Marie lie and say she fell down or walked into something. She would never admit the truth to the police officers or doctors. She always covered up for Manuel.

And he thought he was stubborn! Marie won that award hands down.

"No, it isn't." His father's voice brought Aaron's mind back to the current situation. "But until she's ready, we can only try to encourage her to seek shelter away from Manuel."

"*Si.* I'll be leaving with the kids shortly. They've eaten dinner and will need a good bath." Aaron could hear his father chuckling. He knew his father wouldn't be in charge of baths. "I could have them spend the night at my house tonight so they could swim in the pool."

"Chicken," his father teased.

"Hey, the outdoor shower is a lot easier to clean up." Aaron ended the conversation with his father. "All right, gang, let's pack up our mess, get some clothes from your home, and go to my house. It's a pool party tonight."

"Yeah!" they all screamed and scurried to pick up the debris around their picnic table. With the kids loaded in the van, he drove back to their house. Aaron clenched the wheel tighter as he pulled in the driveway behind Manuel's truck. The day couldn't get any worse. First he lost the contract, then he'd heard about Marie's beating. Then he'd done the most foolish thing of all and kissed Renee. *Renee, of all people. Lord, protect me from myself,* he silently prayed. *And protect me from what I want to do to Manuel.*

❧

Renee cleaned up the office, set the alarm, and left. Would this be her last day working for Sunny Flo Designs? She couldn't work for another man to whom she found herself attracted. *Do I have some sort of weird psycho-thing going, Lord, that I can only fall in love with my bosses? Sounds pretty sick.* Office romances never worked out. She'd heard it ever since entering the business world. But she'd fallen for Brent hook, line, and sinker.

Now she was attracted to Aaron; and while he didn't look or act anything like Brent, he still fit the role of her boss. Of course, she hadn't done anything to bring about that kiss. And she was about to smack him silly for having done such a thing. Why, oh why, had she tried to comfort him? *Ultimately, it's my fault. I should have left the man alone.*

Renee continued to mentally thrash herself throughout the supermarket, down the streets of North Miami, and to her seventh-floor apartment. Once inside, she removed her business suit and relaxed in an old pair of cutoff jeans and a T-shirt. *Hard to believe it's October.* The eighty-degree temperatures seemed more in keeping with early summer than fall.

She flipped open a can of diet cola and went out to her deck. She was several blocks from the ocean with a good view of Biscayne Bay, if she leaned slightly over the edge of the rail. Which she did all too often. Fortunately, it was an easy jog to the beach and the lower campus of Florida State University. The school's property abutted the bay, and it made for a delightful place to run. Tonight she needed to run.

She placed her apartment key in her front pocket and set out at a mild pace. At the edge of the bay, she sat at the water's edge and watched for manatee. She'd never seen the gentle mammal but heard they started migrating north around this time.

"Lord, what happened today?" She paused, waiting for an answer. When nothing came, she continued. "Father, I can't fall in love with my boss. Once was bad enough. I can't put myself through that again."

*I know it was Brent's fault, and he should be the one suffering, yet he's fine. He's happily married. His business is intact. There isn't anything the man lost from our broken engagement.* She'd even been foolish enough to toss his engagement ring back at him. Of course, it had felt right at the time. But she'd die seeing the same ring on his wife's finger.

That's when she'd left. She'd left the job. She'd left the city. She'd left her past behind. And now, it just didn't seem fair to be here in a strange new city with a growing attraction to Aaron Chapin.

She wanted to smack him for being so forward, but the sweet feel of his lips flooded her with passion and desire. Admittedly, she hadn't felt that kind of connection with Brent—ever. Which had made it easy not to give in to his constant demands to have sex before marriage. No, Brent wasn't the best choice for a husband; she saw that now. But it didn't stop the hurt he'd caused her when he'd married another woman without first breaking off their engagement.

Brent Cinelli was a first-class cad with a capital *C*.

She gazed off toward the horizon, where the sky turned the color of orange rose. Renee pushed herself up and ran a couple hard laps on the service road before heading home. She'd have to start looking for another job. She couldn't work for Aaron Chapin any longer.

She entered the apartment to the sound of her answering machine taking a message. "I'm sorry I missed you. I really miss you, Renee. We need you to come back."

Her body stiffened. *Brent? Why would he call me now? How'd he find me?*

That wouldn't be too difficult, she realized. All he'd have to do was contact accounting. They had her change of address.

"Please, Renee, pick up the phone. I want to talk with you."

Her hands trembled as she reached for the phone. "I just came in, Brent. What's up?"

"Oh, Baby, I've missed you," he cooed.

Renee let out a nervous cackle. "Yeah, right. How's your wife, Brent?"

He cleared his throat. "She's fine. I'm just saying the company really misses you. I miss your inspiration. You've put a tremendous hole in our team by leaving, Renee."

"You've got no one to blame but yourself, Brent. Just how long were you going to hide the fact that you'd married someone while you were still engaged to me?"

"I told you I was planning on letting you know," Brent

defended in his nasal tone.

"Of course you were." She bit back her anger. "Get to the point, Brent. You can't charm me any longer." And for the first time she knew the man's spell had no control over her. He meant nothing to her now, other than a sorry man who needed the Lord in his life.

"All right, here's the deal. I need you back here. I'll give you ten grand more than you were making when you left. You'll have full artistic license and at least two assistants doing layout, secretarial, anything you need."

"That's a nice offer. But I have a job. Sorry."

"I'll send you an offer in writing so you can reconsider."

"Brent, the answer will still be no. I'm not interested in your offer. I could never work for you. I don't trust you."

"Ouch! What did I do that was so wrong? Come on, Renee, answer me that. You and I both know our marriage wouldn't have worked. It was for the best."

"You're right, our marriage wouldn't have worked. But I'm a human being with real feelings and didn't deserve to be treated in such a slimy fashion." She stopped herself before she said something she'd have to repent of.

"Well, no matter what you think of me personally, Renee, I always respected your work, and it's your work I want back. Not our relationship. I'll send the offer." He cut the line before she could tell him no.

≈

Aaron worked the kinks out of his back and poured himself another cup of coffee. Memories of Hannah had haunted him all night. Milk swirled in his coffee like the confused images spun in his mind. *Two years, and you're still not over it,* he chastised himself.

He looked at the calendar hanging in the small kitchen. October 4 seemed to stand out above the other dates. "Lord, I still miss her. Has it really been two years?" He placed the quickly drained mug on the Spanish-tiled counter and headed back to the master bathroom for a shower. The pulsing water pounded him, his muscles relaxing in its heat. "Get a grip, old boy. Adam will be awake soon."

Thoughts of his responsibility to raise their son rejuvenated him. His stance surer, he scrubbed his body clean. Wrapping a towel around his waist, he entered his bedroom. There on his bed lay Adam, his black curls resting in stark contrast against the white pillowcase that encircled his head. Aaron smiled at the angelic image. So much like Hannah, yet Adam had some of his own features as well. He slipped on his pants and lay down on the bed beside his son.

"Morning, Adam."

Adam's dark brown eyes blinked, his dimples accenting his smile. "Daddy, I was pretending to be asleep."

"You were, huh?"

"I was going to surprise you."

"Oh, well, I'll pretend to be asleep, and you can surprise me now."

Adam stood up on the bed and towered over his father. "Daddy, that won't work," he said, hands on his hips, confident he knew all the answers in life.

Aaron laughed. "Well in that case, I guess there's only one thing to do." He reached up and grabbed his son, tickling his waist. Howls of laughter filled the room. All the darkness of the previous night faded. Life was here. Adam was the blessing of Hannah's and his life together, merged for all eternity in one little four-year-old boy.

After the tickling match to end all tickling matches ended, he told Adam to go get dressed for the day. And following a gentle tap to his backside, the boy ran down the hall to his room.

"Thank You, Lord, for Adam. Thank You that I still have a piece of Hannah alive and with me."

Dressed, Aaron went into the kitchen and made their breakfast.

"Daddy, is today the day Mommy died?" Adam climbed onto the stool at the counter.

"Yes, Adam, it is."

"Are you going to her grave today?"

"I was planning on it, why?"

"I want to go."

Aaron had never taken Adam to Hannah's grave—the boy had been only two when she died. "I guess you can come."

"Grandma says she's not there, but. . ."

*He needs reassurance she's gone,* Aaron thought. "Sure, Son. I bring flowers, white roses, your mommy's favorites. And then I usually say a little prayer to God."

"What do you pray about?" Adam took a fisted hold of his fork and scooped up some eggs.

Aaron straddled the stool, placing his plate in front of him. "Well, I usually thank God for the time Mommy and I had together and for you. . .and I ask for strength."

"Daddy, why did Mommy have to die?"

"Because bad things sometimes happen to good people, Son."

"But Ricky still has his mommy."

"I know, Son, and I still have mine. Your grandma is my mommy."

"I know that, Daddy."

Aaron chuckled. "Sorry, I forgot you're so grown up now."

Adam puffed up his chest.

"Grandma says Mommy was hit by a car."

*A truck actually.* A knot tightened in Aaron's stomach. He had always been honest with Adam, but he questioned his mother's openness about Hannah's death. "Yes, Son, Mommy was."

"I miss Mommy." Adam forked some more eggs.

"I do too, Son."

"Daddy, are you going to get me a new mommy?"

*New mommy! Where does he get these things?* Aaron wondered. "I wasn't planning on it. Why?"

"On *Barney* they were talking about how some kids have new mommies and daddies, so am I going to get a new mommy?"

*Good grief, how can a purple dinosaur explain. . .* He

broke off his thoughts. "Son, if God sees fit to bring a new woman into my life, then maybe. But I must tell you, I'm not looking to find one."

"Okay." Adam finished his breakfast. After drinking down his orange juice, he leaped from his chair.

Aaron blinked. *What just happened here? The kid is watching too much TV,* he thought. *I need to talk with Mother.* Determined, he cleaned up the kitchen and got ready to leave for work. Adam met him in the hallway, his book bag packed with his toys for the day.

"All set?"

"Yup." Adam grinned.

*How could he stay mad at that adorable face for long?* Aaron mused. "Okay, let's go."

After a brief discussion with his mother revealed that Adam's questions were just natural, Aaron realized he'd been too sensitive. Loss and heartache had filled the previous night. He hadn't experienced a night like that in almost a year. He supposed it didn't help that Marie had left the hospital and returned to her own home with her children. She hadn't appreciated the family's gesture of love and support. She saw it as intrusion. He should have knocked some sense into Manuel while he had the chance last night. Of course, attacking a man in a drunken stupor would prove nothing. Not to mention, Aaron would have a hard time living with himself.

The memory of his little niece, Amanda, clinging to him, not wanting to return to her home, tore at his heart.

At the office he placed a call to the florist for three white roses to be delivered.

Renee was late. It wasn't like her. Would she return? After his inappropriate actions the day before, who'd blame her for never returning? The bell jingled over the door.

"Renee," he called out.

"Mr. Chapin, I believe we have some things to discuss."

He raised his hands. "I know, I know, I'm sorry. I promise it won't happen again. But if you feel you need to find another place of employment, I'll write you the best recommendation you ever had. You're a good employee, Ms. Austin. I don't want to lose you. But I will understand if you need to leave."

She nodded. Her honey hair crowned her head. The feel of her soft, silky locks came back to his mind. Aaron cleared his throat.

"I'll give the matter some thought," she responded. "I was made an offer last night from my former boss."

He never understood why she had left her previous place of employment. She'd only said they had a difference of opinion.

"How is your sister?" she asked.

"She'll be all right. Renee, you're a woman. Tell me why a woman would stay in an abusive relationship?"

"Fear, mostly. Personally, I'd have left the man who laid one finger on me in anger."

She bit her lower lip. Tears pooled in her eyes. Was she going to say more? *Have you been abused, Ms. Renee Austin?* he wondered.

## three

Renee kept to her space in the office. She didn't need to confront yesterday, much less her past, today. As the day wore on, she became more comfortable in the environment. Aaron called her "Ms. Austin" every time he addressed her. Apparently he wasn't about to allow the kiss to destroy their working relationship. And was it really a kiss? Or was it more a man reaching out for something he'd lost?

Amazingly, Aaron seemed under less stress today. She'd looked it up—his wife had died on the fourth of October. Today was the anniversary of Hannah's death. Three white roses were delivered.

"Ms. Austin? Renee?" His voice jarred her. She blinked, seeing him standing in front of her desk.

"Sorry, I was thinking."

"Apparently." He grinned. He held an envelope in his hand. "Here's the letter of recommendation. I hope you don't feel you'll need to use it, but. . ."

"I'll stay for awhile, Aaron, before I decide. I know you were reacting to the loss of your wife."

He scraped a chair across the floor and sat down with a desk between them. "Renee, I'm not—"

The phone rang. She answered it. "Sunny Flo Designs, Renee speaking. May I help you?"

"Hi, is my daddy there?"

"Sure. Just a minute, Adam."

Aaron pushed himself from the chair he'd been sitting in and went to his desk. "Hey, Buddy."

She loved how Aaron treated his son. He was a good father.

"Sure, I guess. Let me speak with Grandma." Aaron sat down. *"Madre."* His words came smoothly in Spanish. Aaron

23

showed his Latin heritage, Renee mused, with his richly tanned skin, dark hair, and brown eyes. But his name was so contrary. He'd explained it once. His father was English, his mother Cuban. And he'd been given his grandfather's first name. The mixture of the cultures within Aaron intrigued her. Intrigued her far too much. She'd been shocked when he'd kissed her. But admittedly, another part of her had wanted that kiss, which was why she knew she'd have to find a new job. On the other hand, they were both adults; they could prevent moments like that from happening. Not to mention, he wasn't really attracted to her. She'd just been handy in a moment of weakness.

Today he seemed like a different man, back to the normal Aaron Chapin. Perhaps she could work through her own foolish attraction and continue working for him. She loved the work. She loved the quality that Aaron strived for. And she loved the integrity he insisted went into each of their products. Not like Brentwood Designs, which cut more corners and churned out more work than anyone she'd ever seen. She'd spend hours of overtime fixing and repairing shabby work. No wonder Brent wanted her back. *He's probably losing accounts without my extra work on the company's behalf.*

"*Si, Madre.* I understand. Tell Adam I'll take him." He placed the handset back in its cradle and rose slowly from his desk.

"A problem?" she inquired.

"No, not really. Adam's growing up. He wants to see his mother's grave."

"Oh." Renee leaned back, crossing her arms, and hugged her shoulders.

"Renee?" he inquired.

"Sorry. I lost my parents when I was eight. The memory of watching their coffins going into the ground just flashed in my mind."

"Adam was barely two when Hannah died. I didn't take him to the funeral. I didn't have the patience for a two-year-old toddler, and I didn't want him having the memory you have."

"You're a good father, Aaron." She glanced down at the

papers on her desk. "Did you find any more purple lines in the presentation?"

"No." He chuckled.

"Good. I went on-line with the old dinosaur computer, and the tennis ball coming at the customer takes a bit to load, but it doesn't run too slowly. I think it's manageable."

"I'll take a look." Aaron went over to the old computer.

Renee went back to work on the coding of yet another Web page. John should be in later in the afternoon to add the color to the logo she'd drawn.

"I agree, it works," Aaron said decisively. "It's almost at that I'm-not-going-to-wait-another-second point when the ball starts spinning at them. Put a message to click the window and move to the next page for those impatient browsers.

"I'm picking Adam up from my mother's after my appointment," he continued, "so I won't be back in today. Would you mind locking up again?"

"Of course not." She should probably protest a little, but what would be the point? She truly didn't mind.

"Thanks, I appreciate it. Have John finish what he started yesterday and whatever you need him to do for you. I'll have a list for him tomorrow."

"Gotcha." *Father, bless Aaron with a sale today,* she silently prayed.

❧

Arriving at his parents' home, Aaron stretched his arms out toward his son, who came running toward him. "Daddy!"

"Hi, Buddy. How was your day?" Aaron held his son chest-high.

"Me and Grandma made play-dough."

"Really?"

Adam shook his little head up and down, then squirmed to get down. "Wanna see?"

"Sure."

The boy tore back through the front door and into his grandparents' house.

*All that energy!* Aaron kissed his mother on the cheek. *"Buenos dias, Madre."* His mother sat with her Bible on her lap in the living room.

*"Buenos."*

"Was he good?"

*"Si,* lots of questions about Hannah and death."

Aaron winced. *"Gracias."*

Adam came running in, a mound of blue dough draped over and around his fingers. "See, Daddy?"

"Wow, looks great, Buddy. Are you bringing it home?"

"Grandma says to keep it here for tomorrow."

"Sounds like a plan. We'd better get going. Put the play-dough away and give Grandma and Grandpa a kiss good-bye."

Adam scurried away.

"Anything I should be aware of, Mom?"

"No. He's just old enough to ask questions now."

"I know." Aaron had hoped this day would never come. How could he explain death to a four year old? He thought back over the years when Adam had asked so few questions about his mother. Taking in a deep breath, he braced himself.

Adam placed his hand into his father's. "Daddy, are we going to Mommy's grave?"

"Yes, Son."

Adam tightened his grip. Once they reached the van, Aaron hoisted the boy up into his booster seat and waved back to his mother. Seat belts in place, he turned the key in the ignition and began the journey of no return.

"Daddy?"

"Yes, Son?"

"Did Mommy's boo-boos hurt?"

Aaron gulped. "Yeah, they hurt, but not for very long."

"'Cause she went to heaven?"

"Yes, 'cause she went to heaven."

"Daddy?"

"Yes, Adam?"

Aaron's jaw clenched at the memory of the car battered and

ripped open, Hannah's blood splattered on bits of broken glass and over the distorted driver's seat. Yes, Hannah did have pain, more than he wanted to tell his son. She had lived for a little more than three hours and died shortly after he arrived at the hospital. His grasp tightened on the steering wheel. His forearm muscles tensed, bracing himself for Adam's next question.

"Did you bring the flowers?"

His pent-up breath escaped with such force, his nostrils flared. "They're up here beside me, Buddy."

"Daddy, why do you bring flowers?"

*Easy question. I can handle easy questions.* "Because your mommy liked white roses. So I bring three. One from you, one from me, and one for her."

Adam wiggled in his seat.

"Son, do you need to go to the bathroom?"

"No." He continued to squirm.

"Why are you squirming?"

"Something's hurting me."

"What?"

Adam reached his little hand under his bottom and lifted himself slightly off the seat. "I can't find it."

"Check your pocket, Son."

He reached into his pocket and pulled out a small ball. "I got it." He held it proudly in the air like a prize trophy.

Aaron smiled. "A ball, huh?"

"I was hiding it in the play-dough at Grandma's."

"Oh."

Aaron parked the van in a shaded parking spot. A few cars dotted the lot. "Here we are, Son."

Adam pushed the button to his seat belt and wiggled out of his restraints. As they walked toward the grave, Adam asked, "Daddy, are all these stones dead people?"

"Yes, Son."

"Why do they use stones?"

"Well, 'cause a stone won't fade away like paint on a sign does."

Adam nodded. "Wow, Daddy, there's zillions of them!"

The boy looked up. "Are you going to die, Daddy?"

Aaron stroked his thumb across Adam's hand. "Someday. But I believe God will have me around for awhile."

They walked hand in hand. Aaron gained strength holding his son's warm, small hand. At Hannah's grave, he went down on one knee. "Adam, this is your mommy's grave."

"What's it say?"

"Hannah Marie Chapin, born January 5, 1974. Died October 4. . ." Aaron cleared his throat. "Beloved wife and friend." His mind ran over the entire Scripture passage the phrase was drawn from. "This is my beloved and this is my friend." A lump stuck in his throat, remembering their wedding day when he had recited that verse to her.

Adam traced his finger in the letters.

Aaron's hand trembled as he placed two of the white roses on the marbled stone.

Mimicking his father's actions, Adam placed his rose. "Daddy, is Mommy happy?"

"Yes, Son. She's in heaven, and it's a wonderful, happy place."

"Does she miss us?"

"I guess so. But it's different 'cause she's with God and feels things differently than we do."

"Daddy, does Jesus give Mommy a hug when she misses us?"

"I'm sure He does." Aaron reached over and gave Adam a big hug. "Hugs are good, aren't they?"

Adam nodded his head. He bent down and patted the stone. "Bye, Mommy."

Aaron's tears burned. "Bye, Hannah," he whispered. "We've got a great son."

❧

Renee looked at the clock. Half past six and she still hadn't left the office. The purple line had appeared on several of her saved files on the network. She'd painstakingly gone through every file looking for any more. She'd never heard of a glitch in software that would cause such a thing. It was peculiar, to say the least.

A bang on the door caused her to jump. She turned to see Aaron putting his keys into the lock. "Is there a problem, Ms. Austin?"

"Hey, Renee," Adam called as he came bouncing in.

"Hi, Adam. No, Aaron, well, yes, actually, but I've been working on it."

"What's the trouble?" He strolled over to her desk.

Adam went over to the old computer and clicked on one of his favorite games.

"Trained him young, huh?"

Aaron's smile lit up his face. "Cheap labor. So, what's the trouble?" He leaned over, looking at her computer screen.

"It's that purple line you found yesterday. It's appearing in several pages of the uploaded files. It isn't on my desktop original, just the uploaded files."

"A virus?"

"Not likely; it's too random. There isn't a logical pattern."

"Let's contact the domain server and change our passwords. Maybe someone got in and has been playing with our files."

"But who? Why?" she asked.

"Probably some kid." Aaron reached for the phone and called the domain server. Within minutes the passwords were changed. Aaron scribbled them down on a piece of paper. "Thanks," he said and hung up the phone.

"Daddy, I'm hungry." Adam rubbed his belly.

"In a minute, Son. Just let me give Renee some information."

"Okay." Adam came up to them and hugged his father's left leg.

Renee smiled. Aaron handed her the small yellow note.

"Daddy, can we go to Chucky Cheese, please?"

Renee chuckled under her breath. Adam always wanted to go to Chucky Cheese.

"What about the peanut place?"

"Peanut place?" Renee wondered where that could be. All

the fast-food places she knew didn't sell peanuts.

Aaron spun around. "Road House Grill."

"Oh." She hadn't meant to speak her thoughts.

"I get a better meal if we go there." Aaron winked. "Not to mention, it's quieter. Although some nights that isn't always the case."

Renee shook her head from side to side.

"Renee, you wanna come?"

"No, I—"

"Dad, can Renee come?" Adam tugged on his father's pant leg.

"Have you eaten?" Aaron asked.

"No, but—"

"Please, Renee," Adam begged. "You put peanut shells on the floor. It's really fun."

How could she turn down the four year old? Her gaze locked with Aaron's. "Are you sure?"

He hesitated for a fraction of a second. "Absolutely."

"All right, Adam, I'll come."

"Yipee. Daddy, can I go in Renee's car?"

Aaron chuckled. "You like that car, huh?"

Adam beamed and bounced his head up and down.

Renee suppressed a giggle. Her Mustang convertible had been a necessity years ago. Now it was a classic in the truest sense of the word. She'd spent a small fortune restoring that car. "It's fine with me."

"I'll put his booster seat in your car, then."

"Sure." She reached through her bag and handed him her keys. Their fingers brushed. Her cheeks flamed. Maybe she should reconsider her position on staying on at Sunny Flo Designs.

# four

The awkwardness of the evening quickly dissipated for Aaron. Renee was a beautiful woman, inside and out. She kept an attentive ear to Adam, yet she didn't let him control the entire evening. Aaron shifted Adam in his arms. The child had fallen asleep on the way home from the restaurant. It had been a very full day, making play-dough, visiting his mother's grave, and having dinner with Renee.

He removed Adam's shoes and clothing, laid him on the bed, and covered him with the sheet and blanket. Kissing the top of Adam's head, he whispered, "I love you, Buddy."

Adam mumbled something unintelligible.

He worked his way back to the living area, pulled out a bottle of water from the refrigerator, and sat down on the sofa, plopping his feet up on the coffee table. Leaning his head back, he closed his eyes. *Father, for the first time I feel I've finally let go of Hannah. It was important to bring Adam to the cemetery. Thank You for—*

The phone rang, interrupting his prayer.

"Aaron?"

"Hi, Mom, what's up?"

"Your sister. I can't get that girl to see reason."

"I can't either, *Mima.* I've tried, but she's just not ready to listen."

"I know but—"

"You needed to blow off steam."

"*Si.* I called earlier. You weren't home. How are you? How did it go at the cemetery?"

Aaron sat back down on the couch. "It went very well. Something happened today, Mom. I finally released her. The burden, not really a burden exactly. . ." He continued to

31

explain about his day and how it had gone.

"I'm happy for you, Son. I know it was difficult. Time does wonders, but you will always miss her. It won't always ache like it has."

At times his mother seemed so wise. He'd never known her to lose someone close to her, not a spouse or a sibling or a parent, for that matter. So how she understood this. . .

He shook his head. It didn't matter. "Yes, that's how it is."

After they finished their conversation, he let out a slow breath and finished his time of prayer with the Lord. "And Father, I don't know what to say about that kiss the other day. She's a beautiful woman, but am I that weak of a man?

"Forgive me, Lord. And help Renee feel safe around me. I don't want to lose her as an employee. She's helped the business in so many ways. I honestly don't know what to do or say."

Aaron clicked on the evening news. The current events rambled on, but his mind kept going back to his inappropriate actions with Renee and how much he wanted to touch her hand during dinner. He'd fought the desire to reach across the table and place his hand on hers. Why?

The blast of the station switching from news to commercials had him reaching for the remote. Lowering the volume, his hand paused. *That's my design!* Someone had stolen his design and sold it to the company he'd been bidding to. "How'd that happen?"

His phone rang again.

"Hello." He watched the screen in disbelief.

"Aaron, it's Renee. Turn on your TV." He heard the excitement in her voice.

"I'm already looking at it. How'd that happen?"

"I don't know. Aaron, I think we have a security leak. We need to get someone to come and check out the system."

"I agree. But who can we trust?"

"I don't know, but don't you have a nine o'clock tomorrow?"

"Yes, but. . .are you suggesting—"

She cut him off. "I'm suggesting that you and I work all night and rethink that proposal. There's no telling how much information has been compromised."

Aaron rubbed the back of his neck. "You're right. I'll have to call my mother to see if she can come here and watch Adam. Then I'll meet you at the office."

"I think we have to work off-line on this, Aaron. I have the entire file, specs, et cetera, on my laptop. We can work from that."

"Would you mind terribly coming here, then? It's already past ten and—"

"No problem. Give me directions."

Aaron quickly ran over the directions and clicked the phone off. He went to his home office and downloaded the working files they had on their site, then promptly disconnected the computer from its on-line service and modem. "Who's doing this, Lord?"

‏&‎

Renee easily wove her way through the city streets. It was quarter to eleven by the time she arrived at Aaron's home. For better or worse, she had to admit the attraction to Aaron. *I'm an adult; this is business. I can control my emotions.* She hoped. She swung her laptop carrying case over her shoulder and marched up to the front door. Her finger poised to ring the doorbell, she paused, wondering if the noise might wake up little Adam. Tentatively, she reached up to knock.

The door opened. "Hi, I heard you pull up."

Aaron's handsome smile totally disarmed her. Perhaps she wasn't as adult as she'd hoped. "Hi, did you put on a pot of coffee?"

He stepped back, opening the door for her to enter. "Better, I put on Cuban coffee."

"I'll be up all night." She grinned.

"That is the idea." He chuckled. "I have a home office. It's small but workable. Or we can work at the dining-room table."

"We'll probably need both."

"True, you can work on layout while I brainstorm over new concepts."

"Sounds good."

He poured her a small cup of Cuban espresso. "Here's mud in your eye." She gulped it down and placed her espresso glass on the counter for a refill.

He knitted his eyebrows. "Are you sure?"

"Yeah, I don't feel a thing yet."

"You will." He poured her the second cup.

As she started to sip, the caffeine from the first took its effect. A sudden jolt coursed through her veins, and she felt like she could ricochet off the walls and ceiling. "Wow."

"I warned ya." He grinned. She noticed he'd only taken a couple sips from his first glass.

"What do they put in this stuff?"

"One of these little shot glasses is like four cups of coffee."

"Oh my."

He chuckled. "Come on, we've got work to do."

For the next few hours they reworked their proposal. By 4:00 A.M. they were printing it out.

"Renee, take a seat and rest for a bit," he offered.

"Thanks. You've got a nice home."

"Thank you. We bought it fairly cheap. It needed a lot of work."

"It's an interesting shape."

"The previous owners made several additions. This section we're in right now is part of the original house. Plus the rooms in the front. The pool and back bedrooms came later."

"You have a pool?"

"Yes, and a Jacuzzi. You're welcome to use it. After a long day at work, I find myself in the Jacuzzi to unwind. Then I cool off with a gentle swim of a couple of laps."

"I'd love to, but I didn't come prepared. You should tell a girl to bring her bathing suit." She winked. *Oh no, why'd I do that? I'm flirting.* She wanted to flee.

"I'll remember that. Renee, we need to talk."

She shook her head. "I. . ."

He came up beside her on the couch, then eased back a few inches. "Look, I don't know why I kissed you the other day. I'm sorry. But I don't think it was strictly as you said, that I was missing my wife. I'd been thinking a lot about her that day, no question. But you're a beautiful woman, Renee. Very beautiful. And I'm not saying that just about your physical beauty, although there is that. You're genuine and sweet. And I love the way you handle Adam. You wouldn't believe how many women have tried to use him to get to me."

What could she say? What did she want to say? "Aaron, I forgave you for the kiss. It's a dead issue."

"Is it?" He reached out, open palmed. She eased hers toward his and pulled it back. He let his hand fall to his side. "Renee, I've been out of circulation for many years, but tell me if I'm wrong here. You are attracted to me, aren't you?"

"Yes. . .no!" She jumped up. "Aaron, I can't." Tears swarmed her eyes. "I like you, but. . ."

He stood up beside her. "I won't force you, Renee. But something happened today. Something very important, and I think you should know."

She raised her head and glanced at him. "What?"

"Please sit. I want to discuss this with you. I promise I won't kiss you or try to hold your hand."

She scanned the sofa and looked back at him. Somehow she knew to trust him. She shouldn't, but she would. Renee sat down on the chair across from the sofa.

He chuckled. "Fair enough. At the cemetery today Adam and I said good-bye to Hannah. A real good-bye. For the first time since she passed away, I felt I had truly let her go. And it felt good; it felt right. I've been so afraid of forgetting Hannah, I've held on to her and her image. Can you understand what I mean?"

She nodded her head. She understood all too well. She'd been afraid to even talk about her parents after they died, fearing she'd remember something incorrectly.

"Tell me about your parents. You said they died when you were eight?"

"Yes. I don't have too many memories. They were sweet, kind, Christian parents who had forgotten to write a will. I was sent to my aunt's house. I always loved my fun aunt Ida when I was a child. But she divorced Uncle Pete when I was six, and well, she never went to church. Drinking, drugs, all sorts of male visitors passed through her apartment. I was her little slave. It wasn't as bad as I make it sound; she loved me in her own way. And she tried, but the alcohol and drugs have a way of making a person less than aware of what they're doing."

"I'm sorry." He leaned back on the sofa.

"Have you updated your will?"

"Yes. After Hannah died, it was necessary, of course. My parents will raise Adam if. . .if something should happen to me."

She rested her head back on the chair. It was close to five o'clock. They were done. She should go home and get some much needed rest. "Aaron, I need to go."

"All right, but what is it you're not telling me?" he asked.

❧

*Stupid, stupid, stupid,* he chided himself. *She's got a secret, and I shouldn't have pushed.* Aaron cleared the coffee cups and napkins from the dining-room table. Placing them in the sink, he stretched his back. Dusk played on the windows. He groaned. Sleep—he needed a couple hours before the nine o'clock meeting.

He sat on the edge of the bed, slipped off his loafers, and pulled off his jersey. His eyes closed, his body fell. Soft, comforting, relaxed. He yawned.

The alarm blared in his ear. His hand patted the end table. One unfocused eye peered at the red digital lights. "Six." He hit the snooze button.

Fifteen minutes later he fumbled for the snooze button and didn't bother to check the time.

He waited for the next alarm. He didn't want to get up but knew he had to. He listened for a moment longer. *It should be ringing now.* Aaron turned his head and peered over his pillow. The lights were out on the clock.

He bolted out of bed and scrabbled to his bureau for his watch. "Argh," he groaned. Ten minutes to nine, and all was not well.

"Adam?" he called, running down the hall to his son's back bedroom.

"Hi, Dad." Adam sat cross-legged in front of the laptop, playing a computer game.

"Do you know what time it is?"

"No, the TV isn't working either."

*Of course not, the power's dead. Which is really odd since there wasn't a storm last night. Must have been a traffic accident on a neighborhood pole,* he reasoned. "Get dressed; it's almost nine, and I have an appointment." *Which I'm not going to make.*

He grabbed his cell phone. All the phones in the house were portable and needed electricity. "I should keep one stationary phone for occasions such as this."

He tapped in his mother's number. "Hi, Mom. I don't have time to bring Adam over. Can you go to the office and pick him up?"

"Sure, what's the matter, Aaron?"

"Power's out. I overslept. I need to call a client. I'll tell ya later."

*"Adios."* His mother's voice calmed his excited nerves.

He tapped in the client's number. "Hello, this is Aaron Chapin from Sunny Flo Designs. I have an appointment with you at nine. I'm going to be a couple minutes late."

"Mr. Reynolds is a busy man, Mr. Chapin."

"I understand that, but there was a power failure at my house, and I'm running late."

"I can't promise, but I'll let him know of your delay."

"Thank you." Herbert J. Reynolds was not one to put off. Aaron would be lucky to even get in the door at this rate. "So much for last night's effort."

Dressed, packed, and in the car by nine wasn't too bad, Aaron mused.

"Daddy, why are we going so fast?"

Aaron glanced at the speedometer and eased his foot off the accelerator. "I'm sorry. I'm behind schedule."

"Daddy, you know you're not 'pose to go fast," Adam corrected.

"Yes, Son." Aaron tapped the steering wheel with his thumbs. He didn't need a four year old reminding him of what he should or should not do.

"Daddy?"

"Yes, Son." He also wasn't in the mood for twenty questions.

"Do you like Ms. Renee?"

"Yes." He took a sideways glance over to his son.

"I like her too. Did you know her mommy died when she was little?"

"Yes," he said cautiously.

"Me too." Adam crossed his feet at his ankles. "Daddy?"

"Yes, Son." Aaron took in a deep breath.

"We didn't pray or eat breakfast this morning."

"No, we didn't. I'll correct that at the office, okay?"

"Okay. Daddy?"

Aaron chuckled. "Yes, Son."

"I love you."

"I love you too, Buddy."

Aaron had to wait for his mother to arrive at the office. Renee hadn't shown up yet. Not that he could blame her. But he hoped it wasn't because of their discussion last night—this morning—whenever. He moaned. He'd been honest about his feelings. The fear in her eyes when he told her. . .

Aaron shook his head. Back in the car, he looked at the now green light.

A horn blared. He eased the gas and worked his way through the intersection. Three more blocks and he'd be there. He parked the car at the first available slot and pulled out the proposal. He didn't have the storyboard, but he did have the laptop. At least he could provide a visual.

Over the next ten minutes, Aaron found himself at the end of a lecture about promptness as a sign of professionalism.

"Mr. Reynolds, I apologize for wasting your time. I happen to have the best proposal you've ever received, but I won't take up your time any longer." Aaron turned to exit the room.

"Mr. Chapin, Aaron, show me what you have. Why was it you were late?"

Aaron gave a brief description of the morning and his need to take care of Adam first.

"Right, you lost your wife a couple years back."

"Yes. Mr. Reynolds, I'd be happy to show you the proposal."

"Go for it." The fifty-something man with white hair and a bulging waistline slipped into the chair behind his desk.

# five

Renee worked the stiffness out of her neck. She'd overslept. The office smelled of stale coffee. She turned on the computers and got to work changing the security passwords for every account. Someone had to be getting in, but how? She clicked through the company's Internet page and found it was vulnerable. In the original coding one could actually get the directories of all the files. So even the files they had protected were visible.

The bell above the door jingled.

"Where's Aaron?" a large-framed, potbellied Hispanic man ordered.

"I'm sorry, he's not here. Can I help you?"

His gaze scrutinized every part of her body. Renee felt like running for additional cover. "You're pretty enough, but I'm looking for Aaron."

"Can I give him a message for you?"

Renee clutched the end of the counter in front of the door and was glad for the blockage.

"Tell him to keep his hands off my kids."

"What?" The word slipped out before she had a moment to check herself.

"He'll know what I mean." He turned and, slamming the door open, left.

Renee watched his lopsided gait. He appeared drunk. She sniffed the air. The scent of stale beer wafted past her nose. Releasing the counter, she slipped down behind it. Clenching her sides, she rocked back and forth. "It's been years, Lord. Why now?"

The bell over the door rang again.

"No, God, no," she silently prayed.

"Renee?" Aaron called out. She rolled onto her hands and knees and pretended to be searching for something.

"Hi, Aaron." She forced a grin and stood up.

"We did it, Renee. We did it." He captured her in his arms and twirled her around.

Renee couldn't help but smile. "What?"

"We landed the account. Thank you, thank you so much." He placed her back down. She stepped back and looked down at her feet. She liked being in his arms. Her heart raced. Why, was it Aaron or, or. . .

"Aaron, you had a visitor. If you can call him a visitor."

"Who?"

"Don't know; he didn't leave a name. Just a message." She paused.

"And?" He placed his hands on his waist.

"He said to tell you to keep away from his kids."

"Ahh, was he in his late thirties, Hispanic, with a crooked nose?"

Renee thought back on the man's features. "Yes, do you know him?"

"Unfortunately yes. He's my brother-in-law, Manuel. Don't you worry about him. I'll make sure he doesn't come by here again. He probably had a few too many to get up the nerve to speak to me."

"He did smell of alcohol."

"Yeah, that's Manuel. I'm sorry you had to deal with him alone." Aaron headed back to his desk, placing his brown leather briefcase on top of it.

"I changed all the passwords," Renee reported, "and I found a way that someone could have gotten to our files."

"How?"

"Our index page coding wasn't set properly, and if someone typed in the right address or rather the right missing word of our address, they could pull up the entire directory."

"No way. I programmed that page myself. I know I took care of that problem."

"Well, I checked the last date that file had been updated. It was about two months ago."

"I'm certain I didn't touch it." Aaron sat in front of his computer and pulled up his daily planner. What was the date and time?"

"August eighteenth, 10:30 P.M."

"That's a Sunday, Renee. I wasn't working here or at home. In fact, I was at my parents' all that evening."

"I don't know what to say, other than I fixed the code and changed the passwords again."

Aaron rubbed the back of his neck. "Thank you. I know it's not your fault."

"No, and I'd say someone's been messing with your work. Thankfully we've caught it in time."

Aaron pulled in a deep breath, causing his shoulders to rise. She could see his neck and shoulder muscles taut. She took a step forward, instinctively raising her hands to massage him. *What am I doing?* She stopped in place and stared at her betraying members. *Thank You, Lord, for bringing me to my senses before I touched him.*

Aaron spun around in his chair and faced her. "Renee, are you all right?"

"Yes. . .no," she stammered. "Aaron, if you don't mind, I think I better go home and get some rest. I don't think I can be productive the rest of the day."

"No problem. You worked plenty of hours last night. Thanks again, Renee. I wouldn't have made the sale without you."

"You're welcome." She fetched her purse and practically ran out the door.

*I shouldn't have picked her up,* he chastised himself.

The door jingled. "Hey, Aaron, how'd it go this morning?"

John ambled over to his desk and plopped his book bag at the foot of his stool.

"Went great; we got the account."

"All right, way to go, Man! How'd they like the logo I came up with?"

John's logo had been put to the side when they discovered their files had been tampered with. But how much should he tell him? Was John the one getting into their system and selling to the competition? But that didn't make sense. He wouldn't need to change the codes because he knew them all. "No, I'm afraid we couldn't use it."

"Huh?" John dropped his pencil.

"Renee and I discovered someone has broken into our files. So we had to come up with a totally new campaign."

"No way, Man. When'd you discover this?"

"Last night."

John whistled through his teeth. "And you redid the entire campaign in one night?"

"Yeah, with Renee's help." Aaron couldn't help but beam.

"You better treat that lady good, Boss. She's a dynamo. I'd hate to see you lose her."

"Yeah, I know." Aaron stepped toward the back room. "Wanna soda? I'm buying."

"Sure, thanks." John leaned over the drafting table and went back to work. He was a blessing, but he didn't have the expertise and developed skills that would come with time and experience. John's raw energy helped keep a project alive, but Renee added to even Aaron's own creative thinking.

"Okay, Lord, I got the message. Hands off," Aaron mumbled and took out a soda and bottled water for himself.

❧

The next week passed uneventfully. Sales were made. Aaron and Renee seemed to work comfortably together, and he'd not touched her in seven days, not even a simple handshake.

"Daddy!" Adam barreled in through the office door followed by Aaron's mother.

"Hey, Buddy." Aaron scooped up and hugged his son.

"Can I stay at Ricky's house tonight?"

Aaron glanced over to his mother.

"Ricky's mother invited him," she explained. Ricky was a year older and lived next door to Aaron's parents.

"A real sleepover, I don't know. Are you old enough?" Aaron teased.

"Dad–dy," Adam emphasized.

"Well? It's a big deal, you know."

"Please, Daddy, please." Adam hugged him again.

"Sure, Buddy." He glanced back at his mother. "Do you need anything from my house?"

"No, Adam and I already packed his bag." She winked.

"Oh, really? Pretty sure I'd say yes, huh?" He tickled Adam on his side.

Adam laughed wildly.

Renee walked in from the back room. "Hey, Adam. Hi, Mrs. Chapin. How are you?"

*"Bien."* Gladys Chapin smiled.

Aaron followed Renee's movements a moment too long. His mother's eyebrows were raised when he glanced back at her. "Aaron, your father and I are waiting on your decision about us taking Adam to Orlando."

"I see, so that's why you agreed to this sleepover."

"Possibly."

He'd been hoping to put off his parents a little bit longer. Adam left for occasional visits with Hannah's parents, but each and every time, Aaron had gotten little or no sleep. The fear of losing his son was so great, he couldn't rest. Hannah's parents had been asking to take Adam for several days, not just an overnight, so that they could bring him to visit some of Hannah's relatives. Aaron knew it was right. He just found it too difficult to be alone and calm.

"All right, all right, you win. You can take him to Orlando."

*"Gracias."* His mother enveloped him in her arms.

"Yippee, I'm going to see Sam!"

"Sam?" Aaron, his mother, and Renee asked at the same time.

"Who's Sam?" Aaron pushed further.

"The seal."

*Okay, I'm clueless,* Aaron admitted to himself. And by the

blank expressions on Renee's and his mother's faces, they were as confused as he.

"Grandma, can we go tomorrow?"

"It's up to your dad."

"Daddy, please?" Adam looked up to him with his big brown eyes and gave him a bright, toothy smile.

Aaron chuckled. "Sure."

"Grandma," Adam said, taking her hand, "we gotta go pack more clothes." He pulled her toward the door.

"Hey, don't I get a kiss good-bye?"

Adam dropped his grandmother's hand and came running back. "I love you, Daddy, thanks."

"I love you too, Son. You mind your grandma and grandpa, all right?"

"Yes, Sir." Adam wiggled free from his embrace and jumped over to Renee.

"Renee, did you hear I'm going to Orlando?"

"I sure did. That's great."

"You wanna come?"

Renee's laughter licked Aaron's ears. "No, I'm afraid I have to stay and work with your dad."

"Okay. Bye, Renee." Adam jumped up and hugged her around the neck. She wrapped her arms around Adam and closed her eyes.

*She loves him. Oh, Father, what's going on here? Why can't we be honest about our feelings? And what are my feelings?*

❧

Renee turned and wiped the tears from her eyes. She loved Adam so much, yet she didn't have a right to feel this way, did she?

Gladys Chapin spoke softly to her son in Spanish. Aaron turned toward her, then looked back at his mother. *"Si,"* Renee understood. The rest of their conversation was a blur.

Gladys kissed Aaron gently on the cheek and tapped it with her hand. *Lord, I miss my mother. How's Adam going to do without his?*

Bringing her attention back to her work, she fiddled with the keys, then went over to John's drafting table.

"What's the matter?" Aaron asked.

"Not sure. Take a look at this." She pointed to the logo John had colored the previous week. "We scanned it in, and I reworked it. But. . ." She shook her head. "It's just not working."

"Let me see." Adam turned and fussed with the terminal behind John's work area. He copied the image and put it in a separate graphics program. "What if we change the color scheme here?" He highlighted the area around the circle and selected a textured color.

"All right, the beige works better, but it's a lousy color for marketing."

"True, but we are in South Florida, and the muted tones work."

"Yeah, but it needs something. That color alone will get lost in the background."

"Right. What if we target this area in the center of the logo and give it a shade of red that will blend with the beige and not overpower it? And let's move it slightly off center. There, how's that?"

Renee leaned over his shoulder, rested her hand on it, and blinked. "Aaron, you're good. You need to do more of the creative work."

"Nah, someone has to make the sales."

"True."

Aaron's gaze shifted to her hand. His scrutiny burned her fingertips. She hadn't realized she'd touched him. "Renee," his voice cracked.

Renee swallowed hard. "I'm sorry."

"I'm not offended. In fact, I rather enjoyed the sensation. Renee, we need to talk. We can't go on like this. There's something between us. I don't know what it is or why it is, but we can't just have it hanging over us. I'm afraid to move and react. I don't know what to do, but we can't keep avoiding it."

Renee closed her eyes. Her entire body started to tremble.

"What? What happened?" he whispered. Gently he pulled her into his embrace. "Shh, it's all right; I promise it will be all right. God will get us through this, Renee. Trust Him."

Tears pooled in her eyes. *Lord, I'm such a baby. What am I going to do?*

Aaron's wristwatch alarm went off. He groaned. "I've got to go, Renee. I don't want to but—"

She stepped out of his embrace. The cool air sucked the warmth from her. His embrace had been so comforting. He grabbed her hand. "Renee, speak to me, please."

She lifted her head and looked into his wonderful chocolate eyes shimmering with flecks of gold. "Later."

"Promise?"

"Yes," her voice quivered. She nibbled her lower lip. Should she tell him?

"Will you be all right? I could call and cancel the meeting."

"No, we've worked too hard on it."

"You're sure?"

"Yes, go." *Now, before I say something foolish.*

"I'll call you." He grabbed the portfolio case and headed out the door. He paused and looked back at her. "Renee, I want to be your friend."

"I'd like that. Bye."

"Bye."

He left. She watched him walk through the parking lot to the van.

"Friendship I can handle, Lord, but this attraction is killing me. Why have I fallen for another boss?" *I must be crazy. I must have some deep psychological need for an authority figure in my life.* Her Psych 101 college course came back to mind. *Maybe I'm pathological.*

## six

Aaron glanced at his watch and tapped his steering wheel. Five o'clock on I-95 on a Thursday night wasn't where he wanted to be. He pressed the autodial of his cellular phone. One ring. Two.

He slammed on his brakes.

Three.

He should have called sooner. His finger went to disconnect.

"Sunny Flo Designs, Renee speaking. May I help you?"

"Renee." He eased out his breath and watched the driver beside him vying for position.

"Hello, Aaron, how'd it go?"

"Fine. I didn't get a definite. They have another company coming in tomorrow, but it looks promising. Come to dinner with me?"

"I don't know."

"Renee, please. We need to talk."

A gentle sigh echoed in his hands-free headset.

"Adam's with his grandparents. We'll have plenty of time."

"Okay, Aaron."

"Great, I'll pick you up at your apartment."

"No," she said a wee bit too quickly.

"All right, where do you want to meet and when?" Aaron glanced in his rearview mirror. Another exit and the evening traffic would be heading in the opposite direction.

"Not Adam's favorite," she laughed.

"No Adam. No noisy kids' restaurant, trust me on that one. I know a great place for steak and seafood. It's on the bay."

"Sounds promising."

"How about I pick you up at the office? Neutral ground, how's that?"

"Aaron. . ." She paused. "That's fine. What time?"

"Seven?"

"Okay, I'll see you then." She hung up the phone before he could say another word. Two hours should be enough time for him to go home, shower, change, and be back at the office, shouldn't it? He hoped so.

The traffic opened up. Aaron pressed the gas and enjoyed the freedom of a nearly empty highway. He autodialed his parents' number.

"Hello?"

*"Buenos noches, Madre."* They spoke for a few moments about Adam, the big sleepover, and the weekend his parents had planned. It seemed unreal to him that in a few hours his parents could have mapped out an itinerary that took in two amusement parks and reservations made at a hotel with a pool.

He drove home, showered, shaved, and changed into a set of casual clothes. Arriving at the office early, he went over the day's work and examined the next day's schedule.

The bell jingled over the door. He glanced up from his computer screen. "Hi, Renee, I was just going over Friday's schedule."

She dropped her purse on the counter. She wore a delicate silk blouse and cream-colored skirt.

"You're lovely tonight."

A faint line of crimson crossed her cheeks. "Thank you."

Aaron stood there tongue-tied.

"Did you see the write-in for the Glickman account at three?"

*Work, a safe subject.* He coughed and cleared his throat. "Yes, I take it they needed to reschedule."

"Yes, but it was rather odd. Their reasons, that is. If I didn't know better, I'd say they had booked an appointment from our competition during our time slot."

Aaron rubbed the back of his neck. Perhaps discussing work wasn't the best solution. "We'll leave it in the Lord's hands, Renee. I don't want to be worrying about it tonight."

She nodded. "I updated your laptop. After last week, I think we need to keep the material close at hand."

"Good idea." He reached for his computer briefcase and left it beside the desk. "I'll leave it here tonight and take it home over the weekend."

He took a tentative step toward her. "Come, let's go before we end up talking about work all night." He braved a wink.

She giggled. "Okay."

❧

Renee found the waterfront restaurant charming. It was set at the end of one of the bridges that crossed the international waterways, better known as Biscayne Bay at this section of Miami. It was obviously built during the sixties' boom. The picture windows looked over the bay, the tables spaced with just the right amount of room between them for some privacy. And the conversation with Aaron had been quite easy up to this point.

He placed the white linen napkin on the table. "Okay, Renee, now that we've talked about everything except what we need to talk about. . ."

She gulped a swig from her water glass.

"What are you so afraid of? Have I done something to scare you?"

"No, it isn't you, Aaron. It's me. My past. . .I'm afraid. . ."

He cupped her hand with his and leaned closer. "No matter what's happened in the past, it is the past, Renee. Jesus forgives."

"I know He does. And I'm not worried about my salvation or my walk with the Lord. It's me I'm afraid of."

He pursed his lips, holding back his thoughts.

"Aaron." She pulled her hand away from his and held both of them on her lap. "I was engaged to my former employer."

His eyelids widened. He sat back in his chair and clasped his hands together, placing his elbows on the arms of his chair.

"Let me start from the beginning. I started working for Brentwood Designs while I was in college, doing much the same as John is doing for you. The firm was larger than yours, but not nearly what it became after I joined the creative team. Brent loved my work. I loved his praise. I found security in it. Eventually we started dating. I put more and more hours into the company, somehow wrapping my relationship with Brent into the need for the company to succeed. Anyway, to make a long story short, as I put more time in the company, Brent put more time in seeking solace from others. He married another gal at the firm without first breaking off our engagement. I won't tell you how I found out."

"Ouch. No wonder you're afraid of us developing a relationship."

She eased out a sigh of relief. "I promised myself I would not fall in love with another employer."

"I see. And do you keep your promises?" His words were tight.

"I try, Aaron." She reached over and touched his forearm. She needed him to understand. "It's not you. It's me. Throughout my entire life, the people I love disappear."

"Renee, that's rubbish. You're letting your experience dictate your actions. Where's your faith? If we're to develop a relationship, and I do mean if, it has to be grounded in the Lord. I trust God to lead and direct that relationship. I can't be anything more than a friend to anyone else otherwise."

"You prayed every time you went out with Hannah?" she asked.

"Yes. I'm not saying that we were perfect. We weren't. We had our problems. But I can't see entering a relationship without God being the center of it. It's too easy to get caught up in a physical relationship, a bad relationship, or anything other than a godly one, without prayer."

Renee closed her eyes. She hadn't put God at the center of her and Brent's relationship. If he hadn't married, she could have found herself giving in to his sexual demands just to keep him. She shook her head.

"What?" Aaron leaned toward her again.

"My relationship with Brent was not Christ-centered."

"Ahh." He eased back. "Renee, I have a son. I can't afford playing with his affections. I can't have him getting too attached to a woman who might not be his future mother."

She opened her eyes and stared into his. Aaron had to be one of the most honest men she'd ever met. "I would never hurt Adam."

He reached for her hand again and caressed the top of it with his thumb. "I know. I've watched you with him. I suppose that is part of what I find so appealing in you, Renee. You love Adam. It isn't phony or put on. And Adam knows it too. He responds to you. Do you know you're the first woman he's hugged outside of the family?"

"Really?" She beamed. *I feel so honored.*

"Really. Kids are pretty sensitive to phony characters. You wouldn't believe the women who've tried to buy him off in order to get to me. Oh, Adam's no saint. He takes the gifts, but then he lets me know he's not very fond of the lady."

Renee chuckled. "Phew, I almost bought him a toy the other day. But I didn't want you to think I was trying to win your affections."

Aaron roared. "You silly woman. You've already won my affections. That's why we're having this conversation. Look, Christmas is around the corner. If you'd like to purchase something for him, you could give it to him then."

"I'd like that." Renee smiled, then grew serious. "Where does this leave us?"

"Answer me one question." Aaron leaned closer.

Renee's heart skipped a beat. Her palms began to sweat. "All right." She managed to squeak the words out.

"Can you trust God to be the center of our relationship?"

"Whoa, nothing like putting a girl in a defenseless position. If I say yes, we go forward with a relationship. If I say no, then I have no faith. You don't play fair, Mr. Chapin."

"Renee, I like you. I don't have time for fair or not fair. I can only deal with straight and open honesty. So tell me, are we going to give this relationship over to God or walk our separate ways?"

"I would like to, but I'm afraid," she confessed.

Aaron took her hand into his and kissed it gently. "Then let's pray about it."

They bowed their heads, and Aaron led them in a prayer. She found herself drawn to his words, drawn to his faith. Could it really be this simple? Did God have a plan for her and Aaron?

She thought about his prayer the rest of the evening. By setting a rule for her to live by, that of not getting involved with another employer, was she limiting God?

Aaron dropped her off at the office, and she drove off in her car. He hadn't pushed for a kiss good night. And she had to admit she had been hoping for one.

"Lord, what's wrong with me? I say I don't want something, and yet I yearn for it. But I have to confess, Aaron is right about our relationship needing to be centered on You. I certainly don't trust myself. Lord, I feel so unworthy of Aaron's friendship, let alone his affections. Please help me."

❧

Aaron looked over at the office. He should probably get his laptop and go over tomorrow's presentation. Turning his wrist, he noted it was already eleven. He yawned. It could wait until morning.

He thought back on his dinner conversation with Renee. *She's hurting, Lord. Help me to be sensitive. Hannah complained more than once about how I didn't understand what she was going through. Help me not make the same mistake with Renee.*

"And, Lord," he continued out loud, "let us know ASAP if we shouldn't be developing a relationship. Give her peace, Lord."

Aaron pulled into his carport and entered the house through the side door. It felt so strange to be alone. "Lord, keep Adam safe."

He retreated to the Jacuzzi, turned on the air jets, stripped down, and left his clothes on the bench in the changing room. Slipping on his bathing suit, he settled into the small pool and let the pulsing water work its magic. What he hadn't shared with Renee tonight was that it was becoming increasingly obvious that someone was working overtime to slander Sunny Flo Designs. The reschedule with Glickman was probably similar to the encounter he'd had today. He'd thought the sale was locked in. It should have been. Today was supposed to be the final presentation. Today he learned Sunny Flo Designs was still going head to head with another offer.

Aaron rubbed the back of his neck and slipped down farther into the bubbling water. At the time he had the Jacuzzi put in, it had been an extra they really couldn't afford. Since that time, the machine had paid off wonderfully by helping him work out the stress in his body.

He angled his left shoulder blade and the base of his neck into the jet stream. He'd injured that spot years ago, and it always seemed like the first area tension started to settle in. He leaned back, closed his eyes, and drifted off to sleep. He woke with the water calming as the jets shut off from the timer.

He glanced at the pool, thought about doing some laps, and looked over to the timer. Should he stay in for another fifteen minutes?

The phone rang, ending all debate.

Who could be calling this late? Adam? The water swooshed as he climbed out and hustled over to the phone. "Hello?"

"Mr. Chapin?"

"Yes."

"Mr. Chapin, this is the North Miami Beach Police. Sir, there's been a burglary at your store."

"What? Why hasn't the alarm company called me?"

"I can't answer that, Sir. I found the place ransacked on my evening patrol. I think you might want to come down here."

"I'll be right there." Aaron hung up, swiped a towel over his body, pulled on a loose T-shirt, and slipped his feet in some sandals. He heard his swimming trunks swish as he walked toward the front door.

"Ahh, phooey." Aaron stomped to his bedroom, dried off completely, and dressed appropriately. Thankfully, he'd come to his senses. Filling out long reams of paperwork in a soggy bathing suit wouldn't have been his idea of fun.

Approaching the storefront office, he couldn't believe his eyes. It looked empty. Wires hung from the ceiling. Papers and posters littered the floor. His heart sank. "What happened?"

A young officer dressed in dark blue walked over to him. "Sorry. I patrolled by here an hour before and nothing looked suspicious."

A detective approached. "Mr. Chapin, I'm Detective Diaz. Can I ask you a few questions?"

"Sure." Aaron had become familiar with the police department after his wife had died. The pending trial on the man who'd killed his wife had put him together with the police department on several occasions.

"Did you have an alarm?"

"Yes, but apparently not a good one," Aaron spat out. He needed to control his temper.

"We'll need to contact the company."

Aaron gave the detective the name of the company. The number was passed to a younger officer. Aaron was certain he'd be contacting the company. "Where's the power box for your system?"

He led them to the back room. Aaron gasped.

"Mr. Chapin?"

"They took everything. Including the safe."

"A safe?"

"I used it to keep backups secure in the event of a fire. It's a fire- and waterproof filing cabinet, not a real safe."

"Was it bolted down?"

"No. Apparently it should have been," Aaron grumbled.

"I'll need the names and addresses of your employees who had keys. It wasn't a forced entry."

"I was with Renee Austin this evening," Aaron offered. He

couldn't help but continuously scan the empty rooms.

"Until the time we called you?" the detective asked.

"No, I dropped her off here around eleven."

"Do you know where she went after that?" Diaz continued to scribble notes on his small pad.

"Home, I presume. It was late." The possible meaning of the detective's question penetrated Aaron's stunned mind. "She didn't do it," he protested.

"I'm sure you're right. Does she have a key and the passwords?"

"Yes. So do John, myself, my parents, any number of people."

"I'll need all their names."

Aaron groaned.

"I also need a list of the items stolen, descriptions, serial numbers, anything that can help us identify your belongings."

*Belongings? My entire office has been stolen, along with my records.* "I have some information at home. I can give you a list of the types of computers, how many desks, chairs, lamps, drafting tables, furniture."

"That will be great, Mr. Chapin." The detective put his hand on Aaron's shoulder. "I'll do my best but. . ."

"I know, I know. Not much gets recovered."

"Unfortunately. It is Miami's largest crime."

Aaron looked at the scattered papers on the floor. A police photographer was taking pictures. Another officer was brushing for fingerprints. Aaron flipped open his cell and dialed Renee's home number.

"Hello," she said yawning.

"Hi, Renee. Sorry for calling so late. I need a favor."

"Aaron, what's up?"

"The office has been burglarized."

"What?" He heard the shuffle of bedcovers.

"After I dropped you off, someone broke into the place and stole everything. Absolutely everything, Renee. I don't even have a seat to sit down on."

"Aaron, tell me this is some sick joke. No, I know it's not. No one would call this late. I'll be right down."

"Thanks. Bring your laptop. Please tell me your laptop is at home, fully updated."

"Yes, I have it." *Praise God,* he had some backups.

"Great. There should be a file in there with a list of all the serial numbers of the computers, electronic equipment, and a few other things."

"Should I bring a printer too?"

"Hang on." He covered the phone. "Detective, can I give you a diskette, or do you need a hard copy?"

"Whichever. I can get it from you in the morning."

"On second thought, Renee, save yourself running out here now. The police detective said he could get the list in the morning. Call me tomorrow, and I'll tell you where to find the files."

"Are you sure? I don't mind coming down now."

"Yeah, I'm sure. Do me a favor, though. Come in tomorrow after placing some calls from your home. I believe I have two appointments, possibly three. Please reschedule for me. At the moment, there isn't even a phone here."

"No problem, Aaron."

"Thanks."

She yawned. "Is there anything left in the office?"

"There are some scattered papers on the floor. But the walls are barren. The place looks like a tomb."

"Oh, Aaron, I'm so sorry. I wish there was something I could do."

"I have it covered. I have to go, Renee. God bless, and say a prayer."

"I will. Good night."

"Night." Aaron snapped the phone shut. "She'll come in tomorrow and bring the list in."

"Great. I have a few more questions."

"Sure." Aaron pinched the bridge of his nose and inhaled deeply. "I need to sit down. Do you mind taking up some floor space with me?"

Detective Diaz quirked a grin. "Why not?"

The next hour passed quickly. The swarm of police and detectives indicated it was a slow night for crime in the area. Aaron sat with his back against the wall holding a Styrofoam cup of stale coffee one of the officers had brought in with him.

Finally it was over. "Good night, Mr. Chapin." The last of the men in blue waved as he walked out the door.

Who had a key? The possibilities were limited. The suspects even fewer. His parents were unthinkable. John had been with him for nearly four years, and nothing like this had ever happened before. That left Renee. *It can't be, Lord. How could she have pulled it off after dinner?*

The detective pointed out that professionals had come in. Even if none of the four with access had been involved in robbing him, they probably gave a copy of the key to someone else.

Aaron shook his head. "It can't be, it just can't."

# seven

Renee found him sitting with his back to the wall, his knees bent and holding up his outstretched hands. One hand held a coffee cup. His head bent down. "Aaron?"

He lifted his head and gazed at her. His handsome smile slid up the right side of his cheek. She gasped. The office stood naked in the bright fluorescent lights. The only thing breaking up the room was the service counter by the door.

"You didn't need to come."

"I know, but I couldn't sleep."

"It's not a pretty sight, is it?"

"No. I can't believe someone would take everything. Computers, yes, but this is insane."

She dropped her keys on the counter and went to him. "I'm so sorry."

"Sorry? Why would you say that?"

A stern look caused her to pause. "I–I." She took a step closer. "I don't know. I suppose it's kinda dumb, huh. Isn't it what everyone says when someone's had some trouble?"

He closed his eyes and nodded. "Yeah, I'm sorry. It's been a long night."

"Apology accepted." She sat down beside him. "What are we going to do?"

"Tomorrow I'll make some calls and get some rental office furniture and equipment. There will be forms to file with the insurance company and a whole host of other things."

She looked over to the door, the various windows. "How'd they get in?"

"With a key and the security code."

"No way. How's that possible?" She placed her hand on his arm.

59

"You've got me. Oh, by the way, a Detective Diaz will be calling you to set up an appointment with him."

"Ah, so I'm a suspect." She winked.

"Apparently. So are my parents, John, and. . .and. . ." Aaron jumped up. "The maintenance company." He flipped open his phone and punched out some numbers.

"Detective Diaz, please.

"Sure, give me his voice mail." She watched him pace back and forth in the empty building, his feet crunching the papers littered on the floor. Methodically, she picked them up.

"Detective Diaz, Aaron Chapin here. I just thought of another group of people who've had a key. The Flamingo Cleaning Company. I don't have their number off the top of my head, but they're listed in the phone book. They've been cleaning my office weekly for years. Call me if you have any questions."

Aaron snapped the phone shut. "What are you doing?"

"Picking up the loose papers. What's this black stuff?" She rubbed her stained fingers on her jean-covered leg.

"Fingerprint powder."

"Oh. Will they need my fingerprints?"

"Yes, if you don't mind."

"No, I don't mind. Aaron, this doesn't make sense. Why would someone steal everything?" She placed the gathered pages on the counter.

"You're right, it isn't normal. Maybe I should have given you the raise John suggested."

*Does he really believe I'm responsible?* "Aaron, you really don't suspect me, do you?"

"No, of course not. I don't want to believe anyone close to me could have done this. However, you are the most likely suspect, according to Detective Diaz."

Tears pooled in her eyes. He didn't believe her, not completely. What had she done to make him doubt? She scooped up her keys. "I'll see you in the morning, Mr. Chapin."

"Renee, wait." He ran up beside her and grasped her elbow.

"That didn't come out right. I'm tired, exhausted even, and have been hit with a horrible situation. Forgive me."

She turned and faced him.

"Please," he whispered. "Before this we started a new friendship. I don't want to lose that."

She didn't either. The thought of them beginning a relationship with God at the center thrilled her. She'd never had that with anyone else. Oh, she had some friends who believed as she did, and they talked about spiritual matters from time to time, but she'd never had a relationship that began with Christ as the center. "I don't want to lose it either, Aaron."

"Forgiven?" His grin took her off guard.

She smiled. "Forgiven."

"Thank you. Seriously, you ought to know that's what the detective was leaning toward tonight."

"I've nothing to hide, Aaron."

"Good, then it's not a problem."

Renee bit down on the inside of her cheek. *Nothing current that I have to hide. They don't need to know about my past. It's none of their concern and totally unrelated.*

"I guess I better go home and get some sleep," Aaron said, "and you should too. We have a full day tomorrow. Besides, you'll get to go shopping. A woman's favorite pastime."

"That's a sexist thing to say." She grinned.

"Maybe, but it's true." He winked.

"I never said I like to shop."

"Come on now, going to the store, buying tons of items and on someone else's credit card? What's not to like?" He wrapped his arm across her shoulders.

"Since you put it that way. . ." She chuckled.

Aaron roared. He clicked off the lights and locked the door.

"What about the alarm?" she asked.

"What's there to steal?"

"I see your point."

He escorted her to the blue convertible. "Thanks for coming, Renee."

His fingers played with her hair. She fought down the desire and compulsion to wrap him in her arms.

"Ah, what can I say. I like the Miami night life," she teased.

"Ah, yes, the girl who comes from New York," he quipped.

"I don't know what you've heard about New York, but in its defense, I lived there for many years and never had anything stolen from me. Of course, I didn't have much to steal."

He chuckled and tapped the hood of her Mustang. "Oh yes, you did."

❧

Aaron woke with a kink in his neck. After two cups of Cuban coffee and a bagel, he began a series of phone calls. He and Renee went over what they still had records of. He couldn't stop chastising himself for having let Detective Diaz plant doubt in his mind about Renee. She worked hard all morning without stopping. By five o'clock, they had three desks, three computers, a printer, a file cabinet, phones, and even trash cans all in place.

The bell jingled over the door. Aaron looked up. "Detective Diaz, did you find them?"

He shook his head. "I'm good, but not that good. I've spoken with the cleaning company, and they're sending me a list of employees and former employees who have worked there. They do have a policy of only letting their foreman carry the keys to the customers' offices. And all of them are bonded and have been with the company for years. But we'll be checking into them as well."

The officer looked around and let out a slow whistle. "You work fast."

"Renee's a genius."

"Is she here? I haven't spoken with her yet."

"She's due back any minute. I sent her to the café for our dinners. You're welcome to wait. Oh, I did find one thing that the thieves missed."

"What's that?" The detective sat in one of the newly rented office chairs.

"My wife framed my first ad, and it's hung in the bathroom. It's worthless to anyone but me, but I'm glad to at least have that."

The thirty-something officer nodded his head in understanding. Whether he truly understood or not didn't matter. It was special not because it was Aaron's first ad, but because of Hannah.

Detective Diaz opened his notebook. "I spoke with your college student."

"John," Aaron supplied.

The officer stopped at the appropriate page. "He was up most of the night with a group of other students cramming for an exam and swears he's never lent the key to anyone. He seems like a decent kid."

"Yeah, he's been working for me for years," Aaron added.

"Your parents I haven't located. Are you on good terms with them?"

Aaron nodded. "Yes. They went to Orlando with my son. Two days' worth of sun, fun, and amusement parks."

The detective closed his book. "How old is your son?"

"Four, and he's quite a little man. He keeps me on my toes."

"My oldest is six and started school this fall. Four was a good year."

"Oh? Is there something I should be prepared for?"

"Girls."

"Girls? At six?" *How absurd*. He prayed the officer was mistaken.

"Let me put it this way. Danny came home from school engaged on his first day."

"What?"

"Seems a little girl named Sam—yes, she's a little girl, I checked on this—caught his eye, or he caught hers, no one's quite sure, and proposed marriage. Apparently Sam's mommy and daddy finally got married, consequently she's real big on engagements and marriage at the moment. My only problem came when he said he had to buy her a ring."

Aaron collapsed on his chair. "I'm not ready for this."

Detective Diaz chuckled. "Neither am I. I did, however, persuade Danny to let Sam know that before a boy and girl get engaged they have to be older and the boy has to have a job."

"I'll remember that one."

"Well, it worked, but only for a couple days. Now Danny wants to get a job."

Aaron grabbed his sides and roared.

The bell over the door jingled again.

Aaron sobered. "Renee, this is Detective Diaz. Detective, this is Renee Austin." He walked up to her and took the dinner bags from her. "He'd like to talk with you," he whispered.

Renee reached out her hand. "How can I help, Detective?"

❧

"I'm sorry you had to go through that, Renee."

"No problem." *The fact that I'm shaking like a leaf has nothing to do with anything,* she reminded herself. In all fairness to the police, the detective seemed to accept her explanations. Considering they were the truth, he should; but one never knew with police, and knowing he was looking at her as the prime suspect made her more edgy than she would have been normally.

Aaron took her hands. "Let's pray."

She nodded.

"Father, we come before You tonight asking that You give Renee peace. And that You give Detective Diaz wisdom. If it's at all possible, bring the criminals to justice swiftly. I sure would appreciate it. You know my needs regarding the missing paper files and other important information, but I trust You to help sort out this mess. In Jesus' name, Amen."

"Amen." Renee took in a deep breath. "Thank you."

"You're welcome. I'm starved. Can we eat?"

"You didn't bless the food," she teased.

He took her hands again. "And Father, we ask You to bless this food to our bodies and thank You for Your provision. Amen."

"Amen." She giggled.

"You're as bad as Adam. He doesn't let me forget either."

Renee laughed, then sobered. "Have you heard from him?"

"Yeah, my parents called shortly after you left for the café. The boy couldn't speak fast enough. He did, however, say the appropriate things and told me he missed me and loved me. A man can live on that for a long time."

She placed the mildly warm plates of food on a desk. "The café said this was your favorite, and they said no charge. They are deeply troubled about the break-in."

"I'll have to thank them later."

Aaron lifted the cover over his meal and laughed. "This is Adam's favorite."

"Oh, do you want me to go back?"

"No, no, it's fine. I order this most often because of Adam, so I guess they probably figured it was for me." He eyed her plate. "What did you get?"

"Pork, black beans, and rice. Want some?"

"No, no, my hot dogs are fine."

Renee let out another giggle. She was on the border of being giddy. Little sleep and lots of stress tended to bring this out in her. She whisked away one of his hot dogs and handed him her dinner.

"Renee, I can eat hot dogs."

"So can I. But I'm not giving up my plantains." She stuck out her tongue.

He laughed. "Woman, you're good to have around. Even a simple meal is enjoyable."

"Wait until you see me with pizza. That I don't share with anyone."

"Oh?"

The playful banter took them through their dinner. Renee looked up at the clock. "Aaron, I know I said I'd stay and work some more tonight, but I'm too exhausted."

"I'm not of a mind to work either. Can I interest you in a swim and a movie?"

"Hmm, big spender, huh?" she teased.

"Truthfully, my credit card will be humming for awhile. The insurance adjuster said it wouldn't take too long, but based on past experience, I know it will be awhile before I receive a payment."

"I was teasing. Ever since you mentioned that Jacuzzi, I've been dying to use it."

"Great, I'll meet you at my place. I'll go by the video store and rent something. What are you in the mood for—comedy, drama?"

*Romance,* she wanted to say, but figured there was no need to go begging for trouble. "You pick. I like everything but horror."

"You're on."

"Should I get some junk food?" she asked. Watching movies always worked up her appetite.

"Wow, a woman who doesn't care how much she's seen eating in front of a man. I'm impressed."

She slapped him on the shoulder. "Hey, I have a boss who works me hard. I have to keep up my strength."

"And potato chips does it, huh?"

"Not the chips alone. It's the salsa, dip, ice cream, brownies, and a host of other horribly good things."

"I can see I'll be doing twice as many laps in the pool tomorrow."

Aaron stood at the security pad. "What's the new code?"

"One, two, two, five, zero, two."

"Oh, right. I'm not sure I'll remember that number. Why'd you pick that?"

"Christmas."

"Christmas?"

# eight

Aaron shut off the outdoor flood lamp after seeing Renee drive off. The evening had been relaxing and enjoyable. He did wonder how she could consume so much junk food and keep her figure. They were learning to be comfortable in each other's company. He went to the poolroom and picked up the discarded towels, then tested the water and put in the right chemicals. Hannah insisted that if he wanted a pool, he'd have to take care of it. She'd grown up with one in her yard and dreaded cleaning it every week. As far back as he could remember, Friday night was the designated night to take care of the pool. Saturdays were generally filled with pool parties or family time.

The pool settled for another week, he slipped into Adam's room and looked at the racing car bed. Soon he'd have to buy Adam a larger one.

The phone rang, and he rushed to the kitchen. "Hello?"

"Changed the locks, huh?"

"Who is this?"

*Click.* The phone went dead.

Aaron hung up and called the police station. "Detective Diaz, please."

He groaned at hearing the detective wasn't working. Briefly, he explained his situation.

"Did you star sixty-nine the call?" the officer on the other end asked.

"No, I called you. Should I hang up and do that?"

"Wouldn't hurt. If you get a number, call me back."

"All right."

He hung up the phone, and it instantly rang again. "Hello?"

"Aaron, it's me. I'm home safe and sound."

"Renee, thanks for calling." Although he wished she hadn't. The number of the former caller was lost.

"I had a wonderful time tonight. Thanks for asking me."

"I had a nice evening too. What are you doing tomorrow?" He leaned against the counter and crossed his feet at the ankles.

"Nothing much. I'll probably go running in the morning, take care of my weekly errands, then put my feet up and read a book."

"Running, huh? I was wondering how you could put that much food away and still stay in shape." He leaned over to the refrigerator and took out a bottle of water.

"Yeah, I've run for years. I love it. Do you run?"

"Nope, I swim, remember?"

"Right. Well in New York swimming isn't always an option."

"One of the blessings of South Florida."

"One," she repeated.

"I was wondering, could I take you out for dinner and maybe persuade you to help me shop for Adam?"

"Shop for Adam?"

"Christmas. I know it's weeks away, but I hate shopping when everyone is running through the store like a madman. And your new security code got me thinking about it."

He heard the purr of her gentle chuckle. "So, will you bail me out and give me a hand?"

"I thought your credit card couldn't handle any more purchases."

"It can't. But I have some cash I set aside for Christmas."

"All right. How about lunch instead of dinner? That way we can eat at the mall and get right to the shopping."

"Lunch is fine, but I'm taking you to a special place in North Miami. It's a truly unique little place."

"What is it?"

"Nope, it's my surprise."

"Okay, tell me this much, do I need to run a couple more miles?"

"Nah, maybe one."

Renee chuckled. "Good night, Aaron. I'll see you tomorrow."

"Night, Renee."

He hung up the phone and fired off a quick prayer. "Lord, help us to keep You central in our relationship."

He headed to his bedroom. The phone rang again.

❧

Renee leaned over with her hands on her knees gasping for air. The sun, salt, and gentle surf renewed her. Running felt good, but she'd pushed herself a little too far. A week of busy work because of the break-in, and now she felt more distant from Aaron than the day less than a week ago when they'd shopped for Adam.

She kept trying to remind herself that the expansive amount of work kept them from having a moment to themselves, but had she been reading more into his friendship? Since that conversation over their first dinner together, had he decided to be simply friends and not be romantically involved? Had she allowed herself to hope too much?

Renee closed her eyes and sat down at the water's edge. "Lord, I'm losing it. I swore I wasn't going to fall in love with another boss and. . .and. . ." She leaned back on her elbows. The warm sand provided a comfortable cushion. "Why do I do this, Lord? Why am I so vulnerable?"

A gull cawed as it flapped its wings flying over her. Another dove into the water and pulled out a small fish. The gentle surf lapped the shore. Virtually alone at this hour on the beach, she decided to run at the water's edge and give herself a harder workout.

Slipping off her shoes and socks, she dove into the water, instantly chilling her heated body. A quick swim rounded out her exercise. Sunset fused the sky with brilliant colors and reminded her she needed to return home.

Lying on her counter was the unopened letter from Brentwood Designs. Brent's offer. Sunny Flo Designs was barely holding its own. Renee didn't know how much longer Aaron could keep her on. Three times this past week he'd lost major sales to another company. What bothered her most was when Aaron came back reporting that the competition had something very similar to her original designs. Who was getting into her head? Had she lost her creative edge?

Putting down the letter, she headed to the bathroom to wash up. She found the shower refreshing as the salt from her swim had already crystallized on her skin and hair.

Last weekend shopping for Adam had been wonderful. Aaron's apparent distancing really left her questioning if she'd misread his signals. After all, he hadn't kissed her or even attempted to hold her hand. Worse yet, he hadn't suggested that she spend some time with him and Adam this weekend.

The phone rang. She wrapped a towel around herself and answered. "Hello?"

"Hey, sweet thing. I left you something."

The phone went dead.

Renee clenched the receiver and scanned the room. Her heart raced. Dressing quickly, she put on her baggy jeans and oversized T-shirt. Taking the portable phone with her, she cautiously worked her way down the hall into the dining area. She sniffed the air. Nothing.

She listened.

Nothing.

She peeked around the corner.

Nothing. Everything was in its rightful place. "What's going on, Lord?"

She stepped into the living area and looked out at the patio. Still she discovered nothing.

Maybe it was a prank call.

The phone rang again.

Renee started to tremble. Should she answer it? *You can't live in fear,* she admonished herself and punched the phone button. "Hello!" She winced hearing the strain in her own voice.

"Renee?"

"Aaron?"

"What's the matter?"

"Oh, probably nothing. I just got a prank call."

"Are you all right? What did he say?" Nervous excitement filled his voice.

"I'm fine. How'd you know it was a man?"

"I guess I didn't. I just assumed. I had a caller last Friday night."

"You did? Why didn't you tell me?" *Not that he has to tell me everything. . .but it would have been nice to know.*

"Call the police. Did you star sixty-nine the call?"

"No, it just happened. I suppose this will sound dumb, but I was searching my apartment."

"What did he say?" Aaron's voice rose.

She repeated the caller's message.

"I'm on my way. Keep the doors locked until I get there."

"Aaron, I'm fine. Seriously, I'm okay."

"I'm sure you are, but I was calling to see if you wanted to join Adam and me for pizza. I know that's your favorite meal."

Renee chuckled.

"Also, we were hoping to convince you to come to the zoo with us tomorrow."

"The zoo?"

"Yeah, you know the place where we can see wild animals safely at a distance."

"Sounds like fun, and I haven't eaten dinner yet." She continued to scan her apartment looking for anything out of place.

"Good, because we already have the pizza. And I'm only a block away."

"Pretty sure of yourself."

"You betcha. Renee, I've missed you. It's been a crazy week, and we haven't had a moment to ourselves. I want to spend some time with you. Do you mind?"

Renee closed her eyes and swallowed back the tears. She'd

been hungering for the same thing. Maybe this relationship could work. *God, help me to trust You here.* "No, I've missed you too."

"I'm pulling into your parking area now. Adam and I will be right up."

"Okay." *Oh no.* "Aaron, wait, I'm not dressed." She heard the buzz of the disconnected phone. "Ugh."

She ran to her bedroom. *Presentable clothes, I need presentable clothes.*

The doorbell rang.

She looked at her baggy clothes in the mirror and groaned. *Oh well, I'll lose him for sure now.*

"Renee," she heard Adam squeal. He ran toward her as soon as the door was open.

"Hey, Buddy, how was Orlando?"

"Cool. I had so much fun."

"You'll have to tell me all about it."

She looked up at Aaron, who was holding two pizza boxes in his hand and wearing a frown. She caught his gaze looking to the right of her door and followed it. "What on earth?"

❧

Aaron let Renee occupy Adam while he stood outside the apartment and called the police. The thief had returned some of her personal items from the office in a box beside the door. Thieves never returned stolen items. Something wasn't adding up.

Aaron told the officer what he'd discovered at Renee's. Detective Diaz agreed to come over and treat the box and the surrounding area as a crime scene. Having sheltered Adam from the break-in at the office, Aaron didn't want to discuss this new development in front of him. Hopefully the pizza and the video he'd rented would do the trick. Meanwhile, he'd wait for the detective outside to keep his arrival from distracting Adam.

A short while later, the officer stepped out of the elevator. "Detective Diaz, thank you for coming." Aaron extended his hand. Fifteen minutes, not bad for a police response.

"Has Ms. Austin verified the items?"

"At a glance, yes. We didn't want to touch them in case you could lift some fingerprints."

"Wise decision. You mentioned on the phone she received a phone call first. Were you here at the time of the call?"

"No, my son and I were on our way. Detective, I've tried to keep most of this from my son. He's in the apartment with Renee. Is it possible to speak with her privately?"

"Of course. Please send her out so we can talk."

"Certainly."

Aaron went inside the apartment. "Renee," he called. He'd never been in her apartment before. Sparsely decorated but functional seemed the best way to describe it.

She came up beside him. He grinned. She'd changed from the baggy clothes. "You look good."

"Thanks." Her cheeks stained with crimson.

"You're not used to people giving you personal compliments, are you?"

She shook her head no.

He reached for her and embraced her. "Get used to it. I think you're kind of special and definitely beautiful."

He felt her relax in his arms. An urge to protect her washed over him. "Detective Diaz is outside wanting to speak with you," he whispered.

"Okay, I'll be back as soon as possible. Adam's in front of the television watching the movie you brought."

"Thanks. Call me if you need me." He squeezed her hand tighter and released her from his embrace.

Aaron followed the sounds of the television and sat down on the couch beside Adam. "Daddy, will the police fix Renee's things?"

*Fix?* "*Si,* they'll make it all better."

"*Bien.*"

Aaron grinned. "*Mucho bien,* Adam. You've been practicing."

"*Si,*" he said as if he'd been speaking Spanish all his life.

Aaron chuckled and rubbed his fingers through Adam's curls.

Twenty minutes later Renee came back in and paced back and forth in the kitchen. Her clenched jaw spoke volumes. "He'd like to speak with you again," she said softly when Aaron came over to her.

"Are you all right?" He reached out and placed his hand on her shoulder.

"I will be. The man is going to drive me to drink, I swear. He's so accusing. Do you know he suspects me of planting that box on my doorstep?"

"He accused you?" Aaron's anger rose.

"Well, he didn't say the words, but that's what he was hinting at." She lowered her voice. "I'm sorry. I know it's the man's job, but really."

Aaron nodded his head. "I'll take care of it." It was time for Detective Diaz to get something straight about Renee. He caught himself before slamming the door shut on the way out.

"Why are you accusing Renee?" he asked the detective directly.

"I'm not. I have to look at all angles. And why didn't you tell me that you and she were having an affair?"

"You wait just one minute. I'm not having an affair with Renee. We are friends. Nothing more, nothing less. And this friendship has increased in the past couple weeks, but that does not mean we're having a sexual relationship. Do you think I'd be so stupid as to do such a thing in front of my four-year-old son?"

"Trust me, you don't want to know what others do. Look, I apologize for the affair comment. But you have to try and see things from my perspective for a moment. Your relationship with Ms. Austin clouds your judgment. I'm not saying that is bad or good judgment, but it clouds it, and I need to take that into consideration while I'm investigating a crime. This crime was personal. Thieves don't take everything. At least not normally. This is not your normal case."

"You're right, but do you have to be so rude to her? I know

her. I know she isn't behind this."

"Look, I know you think you know her. But are you aware that she was once engaged to her former employer?"

"Yes."

"Oh. Well, did you know that engagement ended because she was too controlling and demanding?"

"That's not how I heard it. The man is a genuine sleaze. He married another woman without breaking off his engagement with Renee."

"Interesting."

"Did you ask Renee about this?"

"Yes. She wasn't as forthcoming."

"No, I imagine she wasn't. She's a rather private person. Did you tell her what Brent told you?"

"No. Look, I'm not on trial here. Renee is the one under investigation. She's still a suspect, and the fact that these items have shown up at her home says one of two things. Neither of them is very pretty."

Aaron took in a deep breath and counted to five before asking, "What are you suggesting?"

"One, that she's in on this, and with your own admission, she didn't know you were coming so she didn't have time to hide the evidence. Two, that the thief may want something more than the contents of your office."

"I don't believe this. I can't."

"Look, you can't go by your emotions here. You have to look at the facts."

"And you saw proof that she did this?" Aaron inquired.

"No, just Mr. Cinelli's word."

"And you trust that slime ball?" Aaron rubbed the back of his neck. "Look, I'm not trying to tell you your job. But Renee's been putting in tons of overtime for me. She's found areas where our company has been vulnerable. Someone's been stealing our ideas, and she's managed to help prevent some of it."

"What do you mean, someone is stealing your ideas?"

"I've lost a couple of sales lately, and one of the companies that didn't go with our design actually used our design in an advertisement recently."

The officer tapped his notebook. "Can you prove someone's been stealing your work?"

"Not now. My computers were stolen, remember?" He didn't hold back the bite in his words.

"Look, maybe your Ms. Austin is as pure as she looks, and if she is, she is vulnerable. This thief, whoever he is, knows where she lives. Does she have a security system?"

"I don't know. This is the first time I've been inside her apartment." Aaron felt a cold sweat wash over him. Renee was in danger. *Why?*

## nine

Renee grabbed the porcelain sink and stared at the reddened reflection of herself. Brent had lied to the police, leading them to believe she was the primary suspect. Aaron's anger had hung just under the surface when he'd come back in and told her. She fought down her own. Adam didn't need to see her upset. *Help me calm down, Lord,* she prayed. The small bathroom worked well as a place of solace.

She sighed at her reflection. She and Aaron could talk later. For now they needed to forget the past hour and enjoy the remainder of the evening. A cool damp cloth held to her face helped to remove some of the pink, and she prayed once again to calm down.

Renee put spring into her step and bounced out of the bathroom with a plastered smile.

"I'm really hungry, Renee. Can we eat now?" Adam pouted.

"Sounds like a good idea to me, Sport. What about you, Aaron?" She winked at him.

"Better watch out, Adam. Renee loves pizza. She'll eat your piece if you're not looking," Aaron teased.

"I wouldn't take Adam's piece, but I'd take yours." She ran toward the table.

Adam ran after her, giggling. Aaron groaned as he got up and followed them in. "I bought two. Figured one for you and one for us."

Adam's large brown eyes stared up at her. "You eat a whole pizza, Renee?"

"Sometimes, but today I don't think so."

"Wow, Daddy, I never saw someone eat a whole pizza before."

The three of them laughed, the strain momentarily broken.

They enjoyed the evening together in spite of the constant undercurrent of tension in the background. Aaron had to be filled with tons of questions. What had the detective told him that he hadn't told her? Should she make an appointment to lay everything out for Detective Diaz? Having her word challenged had always been something she fought. She'd seen an aunt who lied to everyone. Her parents, what little she could remember of them, had always been honest with her. She tried to live her life after their example.

Aaron lifted Adam into his arms. The poor boy was dragging but hadn't fallen asleep. "I'll call you," he whispered.

"I'll be here."

He reached out and held her hand. "Get some rest, Renee. The zoo will wear you out."

"Oh?" At least he believed her. She smiled.

"Good night." Aaron squeezed her hand.

"Night. Good night, Adam." She leaned over and gave him a kiss on his cheek. The boy's eyes fluttered. "Take the poor boy home. Call me after he's settled."

"I will. Bye."

She waved them off and watched them until they stepped into the elevator, then closed the door. She turned to clean up the kitchen, then realized she hadn't latched the dead bolt. Correcting her mistake, she marched into the kitchen, pulled the phone down from the charger, and immediately called the police.

"Detective Diaz, please."

"One moment," the female voice responded.

"This is Detective Diaz. How may I help you?"

"This is Renee Austin. I think we need to have a talk."

"Oh? Is there something you forgot to tell me?"

"What I'd like to tell you and what I'm going to tell you are two different things. First, I won't say what I feel because I'm a Christian and the Lord wouldn't be pleased with me for saying such things. Second, there's obviously been some sort of problem with Brent Cinelli's memory if he's telling you that I've been carrying a torch for him. I've been angry at him, no question, but it's not because I'm so desperately in love with him that I can't see myself living without him. In fact," she emphasized and took another breath, "sitting on my counter is an offer from him to come back and work for him. Doesn't that sound strange if I'm supposedly chasing after him?"

"First, calm down, Ms. Austin."

"I am calm," she protested.

He coughed.

"Oh, all right, I'm steamed. But I'm being accused of something that isn't true. What can I do to correct the situation?"

"For starters, I'd like to see that letter."

"I haven't opened it." Renee held the envelope in her hand.

"Perfect, then we can open it together, and I will know for certain you didn't forge the documents inside."

She dropped it back to the counter. "You actually think I'd do that?"

"Look, I've done a check on you, Ms. Austin. The most I've come up with is a New York State driver's license. By the way, did you know you're supposed to get a driver's license from Florida within thirty days of moving here?"

"Yes, I just haven't had time. Are you going to arrest me for that?"

He chuckled. "No. But I'd like to see your Florida license by the end of next week."

Renee groaned. "Fine, I'll skip work for a day and get my license. Happy?"

"Some. Look, I know you and Mr. Chapin seem to have a more personal relationship, and this business with Mr. Cinelli makes for some interesting suppositions."

"Trust me, you haven't gone anywhere with the Psych 101 on that one that I haven't gone myself. Look, I'll fill you in with all the horrid details of my relationship with Brent if I must, but I can't prove my story over his. And I doubt there's anyone working for him at the moment who would dare say anything contrary to what he's said."

"Are you saying his employees lie for him?"

"I'm saying he calls it company loyalty."

"I see. And what about you, Ms. Austin, what do you call it?"

"I call it lying, and I wouldn't do it for him. I wouldn't answer some questions sometimes, but I'd never lie for him. He knew that and kept me from the customers he was being less than honest with."

"I see. Are you saying Brentwood, Inc., is less than honest in its business dealings?"

"No, I'm saying that from time to time Brent would encourage folks to agree with what he said. He's a salesman, and sometimes salesmen exaggerate their claims. I would stay late into the night trying to work some of the miracles he claimed the Web pages would do. At the time, I figured I was investing in Brent's and my future. We dated for two years. He told me that when we married, I'd be a joint owner."

"Is that why you agreed to marry him?"

She let out a strangled groan. "No. I thought I was in love with him. The fact is I was in love with the idea of getting married. The ugly truth, as I look back on it now, is that it didn't matter who that man was, as long as I found a good and stable husband."

"Why was that so important for you?"

"Because my parents died when I was eight, and I was forced to live with my aunt, who had more men than I can remember. It wasn't a pretty life, Detective. I'm sure in your line of work you've seen plenty of children who had alcoholic, drug-addicted prostitutes for parents."

"I'm sorry. I can come over in thirty minutes—if that isn't too late for you?" he offered.

"Thirty minutes is fine." The call waiting rung in her ear. "I've got another call. I'll see you then." She clicked the phone and answered. "Hello?"

"Hi, he was out cold before I got to the house. I almost turned around so we could talk. Renee, I'm sorry about what

Detective Diaz said to you."

"It's all right. It's his job, I guess."

Aaron snickered. "It might be, but I'd like to see the man use a little more common sense." He used his toes to remove his shoes and then placed them under the bed.

"I don't know why Brent said those things," Renee said. "It doesn't make sense."

"No, I suppose it doesn't." He took in a deep breath and returned to the kitchen, pulling out a bottle of water from the refrigerator. "You know, the Jacuzzi is here if you'd like to sit and relax."

She groaned. "I'd love to, but Detective Diaz is coming over in a few minutes."

Aaron's back stiffened. "What for?"

"I invited him to. I'm going to tell him every single thing about my relationship with Brent. He'll probably be bored to tears by the time he leaves."

Aaron chuckled. "I'll pray for you."

"Thanks, you don't know how much it means to me, Aaron."

"You're welcome. Renee, can you come to my house in the morning? Then we can leave right away for the zoo. Adam loves it there and, trust me, we'll be exhausted by the end of the day."

"How about if I bring breakfast?"

"What do you have in mind?"

"Fast food, totally not nutritious." She giggled.

Aaron grinned. "Adam will love you. Personally, I like donuts with lots of fillings."

"I'll remember that."

"Renee, for what it's worth, I believe you."

"Thanks, that means a lot."

"You're welcome. I'll be praying that Detective Diaz sees the truth and moves on to the right suspects. Although I'm totally clueless. Why would they return your personal stuff to you? It doesn't make sense."

"It doesn't, and nothing they returned was that personal. I don't have much in the way of keepsakes or memorabilia."

Aaron stretched. "I better get going if I'm going to have all my work done before the zoo tomorrow."

"Don't stay up too late."

"I won't." A desire to say he loved her overwhelmed him, but reason won out. "Good night, Renee."

"Night, Aaron."

He placed the phone back in the charger, walked to his office, rolled his shoulders, and connected the computer to download. While he was on-line, he decided to check out a few Web sites he'd been bidding on to see what the competition had come up with that he'd lost to.

The first page loaded. His eyes widened. "No way!"

He typed in another page. Anger, frustration coursed through his veins. He picked up his cellular phone and dialed.

❧

"Excuse me, Detective Diaz," Renee said as she turned to answer the phone. "Hello?"

"Renee, it's me again. I'm on-line. I've found something very disturbing."

"What's the matter, Aaron?" She glanced at the detective, his interest piqued.

"Can you go on-line right now while you're on the phone?"

She heard something in his voice—frustration, anger, she wasn't certain which. "Sure. Detective Diaz is here. Do I need to do it now?"

"Good, he'll need to see this too. You can explain to him what he sees."

"All right. Would you like to talk with him?"

"Sure, put him on the line."

"Okay." She cupped the phone and said, "Aaron would like to speak with you. He has something he'd like us to see on the Internet. I'll boot up my computer." The detective nodded.

"Detective Diaz. What can I do for you, Mr. Chapin?" she heard him say as she went to her desk in the dining area.

*What had Aaron so troubled?* she wondered.

"I'll make the contact. Let me see the evidence first." The detective walked toward her with the phone. "He'd like to speak with you again."

"Hi. You're scaring me, Aaron. What's the matter?"

"Honey, you'll see in a minute." *He called me Honey.* Her heart warmed, and her nerves calmed.

"Okay, the computer's just about booted up."

"Good." His voice quieted. "Connect and go to the jaja.com site."

"All right." She paused, then gasped. "Aaron, how'd this happen?"

"I don't know, but I think someone got into our system long before we realized."

Tears pooled in Renee's eyes. Detective Diaz looked over her shoulder as she pointed out the various Web sites she and Aaron had bid on. Five sites had nearly identical copies of what they had put together. Too identical. No one could come up with the exact designs they had. No one.

*Once maybe, but five times? No way.*

Renee ended the phone conversation with Aaron, and the detective took a seat and patiently listened while she explained what she'd done, how the Web page coding was even the same.

"I don't know enough about computers, but I have a good pair of eyes. There's no question those are your designs."

"I can't believe they had access to our system for so long."

Renee tapped in another address. Remembering Aaron's anger, she fired off another prayer for him.

"Do you have records on your computer that prove you made these designs?"

"Yes." She opened the window to the file folder for all the projects she'd worked on for Sunny Flo Designs. She groaned.

"What's the matter?" the detective asked.

"All the files have the last date I opened them. They were

reloaded onto the new computers after the break-in. All the dates are wrong."

"What about backups?" he asked.

"They were kept at the office." She nibbled her lower lip. "Wait, there may be a record of some sort in the history file from the Web browser. It shows when a file was opened. . .the name of the address and the date. Bingo. Here's your proof." Finally something was going right.

"Can you give me a printout of that? And a list of your files?"

"Sure." Renee hit the appropriate keys, and the printer hummed to life.

"While that's printing, let's open that letter you received from Mr. Cinelli."

"Sure. That's odd."

"What?" The detective leaned toward her monitor.

"The designer of the Web page isn't listed on the page. No one designs pages without having a link back to their business page. It's a form of advertising. Unless the customer pays a huge fee for not putting it on their page."

"Consequently, we don't know the name of the company that's stolen your designs?"

"You've got it."

"Okay, show me that letter."

She thought she heard hope in the detective's voice that she wasn't guilty. "Here." Renee handed it to him.

"Go ahead and open it," he encouraged.

She supposed it was a federal offense to open someone else's mail. *Who would charge him for it?* she mused. Taking in a deep breath and letting it out slowly, she slid the metal blade of the letter opener up the envelope. Inside was a cover letter followed by a two-page contract.

"Here, as I said, is Brent's latest offer to me. Please note, I'm not chasing him; he's chasing me down. Not personally, just professionally." The detective scanned the various pages. "As I said on the phone, I did a lot of extra work for him, fixed a lot of problems he was even unaware of at the time. Now I imagine he's realizing just how much I did to keep that office running smoothly."

"He says here that he'd spoken with you on the phone about this."

"Yes, he called. I generally don't pick up when I know it's him but. . . You know, I think that message might still be on the tape. I didn't erase it. I don't have many calls." Renee stepped over to the counter with the answering machine, rewound the tape partway, and listened. A message from the cleaners saying her laundry was done filled the silence. "It was before this message." She pushed down the rewind key again. Counting fifteen seconds, she stopped it and listened. Brent's whining voice came on the tape. "Oh, Baby, I've missed you."

Renee grinned. Not only was his message there, but their entire conversation had been taped. She'd forgotten to turn off the machine.

"Interesting," Detective Diaz said after hearing the entire conversation. "This does paint a different story than what he claims. Can you tell me what's in your sealed juvenile record?"

Blood pounded in her ears. He'd found it. She paled. "It's sealed for a reason, Detective," she replied, her voice tight. He didn't need to know; no one needed to know. Why would he even ask?

# ten

A sigh of pleasure escaped Aaron's lips as he leaned back into the jet stream of the Jacuzzi. He hadn't planned on a seven o'clock wake-up call from the FBI. *It seems Detective Diaz doesn't sleep. When the man gets ahold of something, he goes at it like a shark on a feeding frenzy.* Monday morning Diaz would meet them at an agreed-upon spot. Maybe the accounts were lost, but Aaron might still see some justice come from this.

Resting his head on the rail, he put together a plan to make the company's computer system completely separate from outside lines. He wouldn't be taking any risks during the next few months. He couldn't afford it.

"Hi, Daddy!" Adam stood in his pajama shorts and overstuffed truck slippers.

"Good morning, Son."

"Are we going to the zoo?" He placed his hands on his hips.

Aaron fought down a chuckle. "Yup, I'm just relaxing before you wear me out today."

"Daa-dy, we're just going to the zoo," he protested.

Oh, to be four when your biggest problem was going to the zoo. "Wanna come in?" Aaron tapped the water for emphasis.

"Will we still go to the zoo?"

"Of course. And the zoo isn't open yet, so we have plenty of time."

"Okay." Adam ran to the changing room.

Aaron chuckled as he heard the thumping of the boy struggling to remove his slippers.

"Dad?" Adam called.

"Yeah, Son."

"When's Renee coming?"

"She should be here around nine."

"Ta-da!" Adam jumped out and posed with his superhero bathing trunks on.

"Hey, Buddy, come on in." Aaron waved him over.

The doorbell rang. "I'll get it," Adam squealed as he ran out of the pool room and down the hall faster than Aaron could open his mouth to speak.

"Dad," Adam hollered. "It's Renee."

Aaron glanced at his wrist. She was early. She probably hadn't slept well either. He stood and stepped up out of the Jacuzzi.

Renee's warm smile applied a soothing balm of healing over his ragged nerves.

"Hi." He returned her smile.

"Hi. I brought semi nutritious and definitely not nutritious." She held a fast-food bag with the smell of ham-and-egg sandwiches and a long box with at least a dozen donuts.

"How hungry are you?" he teased.

"Now, before you jump down my throat for my weird eating habits, there are four of the basic food groups in this bag. The box contains the necessary food group for the soul."

"The soul?" He grabbed a towel and started to dry himself off.

"I'm hungry, Daddy. I want the donuts." Adam beamed.

"After you eat the egg sandwich." He winked at Renee.

"I'll set the table while you dry off. Do you have orange juice?"

"Yup, and coffee should be just about ready."

"Great. Come on, Adam. You can help me."

"Okay." The boy followed her into the kitchen. She was good with Adam, and it gave Aaron a sense of peace to continue going forward with their relationship. No matter what Detective Diaz claimed.

Making quick work of changing, he readied himself for a day at the zoo—a pair of shorts with lots of pockets. He always needed pockets when he took Adam places. Adding a comfortable pair of sneakers for extensive walking and a light jersey top, he glanced in the mirror and ran a quick comb through his damp hair.

"What kind of jelly donuts did you buy?" he asked, entering the dining area.

"Blueberry, strawberry, cream, and spiced apple," Renee answered, giving Adam the napkins to place on the table.

"What can I do?" Aaron asked.

"Sit yourself down and eat. Adam and I have everything ready."

"Good job, Buddy," Aaron praised and extended his hands for Adam and Renee to pray with him over their morning meal. "Father, thank You for giving us a great day to visit the zoo. Bless us and keep Your protective hedge over Marie and her children."

Adam added, "And God bless Grandma and Grandpa and Nana and Papa."

Aaron gave her hand a slight squeeze of reassurance. Renee cleared her throat. "Lord, thank You for bringing Adam and Aaron into my life. May I be as good of a friend to them."

Aaron concluded. "In Jesus' name, amen."

The prayer over, they all dove into their egg sandwiches.

"Renee?" Adam mumbled.

"Adam, don't speak with your mouth full."

"Sorry." He swallowed a huge amount. "Renee, have you been to the zoo?"

"In the Bronx."

"The Bronx, where's that?"

"In New York." Aaron found himself watching her every move, like the delicate way she wiped her mouth with the napkin.

"Oh, where you used to live?" Adam asked.

"That's right."

"What's your favorite animal? I like the elephants and their big floppy ears. But the lions roar real loud. Wanna hear?"

"Sure." Renee smiled.

"Roar!" Adam yelled.

"Oh my, you sound just like them. Can you sound like a monkey?"

The next few minutes passed with each of them imitating animal noises. The sandwiches done, Renee opened the box with the delightful array of sin to the waistline or backside— Aaron never was sure which. Either way, it meant more laps in the pool. Of course, he'd be doing some serious walking today. . . . Aaron took two.

Renee giggled but kept her comments to herself. He supposed she had a right after the way he'd ridden her case last night about the pizza.

"I'm done. Can we go now?" Adam's smile, accented with powdered sugar and strawberries, broadened.

"I think you need to wash your face, Buddy. Then you'll need to get dressed for the zoo. Wear shorts and a T-shirt, and don't forget your backpack."

"Okay." Adam's jelly-stained hands grabbed the back of the chair.

Aaron groaned.

Renee jumped up. "I'll take care of it. I brought the messy treat."

Aaron pushed his chair back and gathered the paper debris. They collided as Renee came out of the kitchen. "Oof."

"Sorry," she said, stepping back.

"How are you this morning?" he asked in a whisper.

"All right, I guess. I spent several hours looking for any other customers that we bid on. But I think you found them all."

"It's disturbing, but I don't want to discuss work today. I'd rather focus on more pleasant things, like Adam and you."

Renee's cheeks instantly blushed.

"Do you know you produce the most beautiful shade of pink?" He winked.

The blush deepened. Desire surged through him to wrap her in his arms and kiss her senseless. "Are you prepared for today with some sunblock?"

"Ah, um," she fumbled over her words. "Yes, why do you do that?"

"Do what?"

She placed her hands on her hips. "Look, I might not be the brightest when it comes to male-female relationships, but I know you were. . ."

"Come here," he cooed, pulling her to himself. Raking his fingers through her golden strands, he placed one hand behind her neck and tilted her head back. "May I?"

She blinked. He prayed it was a yes. Slowly he lowered his lips to hers. Her arms wrapped around him. He wrapped his around her. Desire and passion fused with a mind-numbing sensation, rendering him unaware of anyone, anything, other than Renee. His hands caressed her shoulders. The kiss deepened.

"Daddy, are you kissing Renee?" Adam giggled. The world, reality, came crashing back down. Aaron pulled away and stepped back.

Stunned, Renee opened her eyes. How could she and Aaron have forgotten that Adam was in the house? How could they have gotten so lost in that kiss? Renee sighed and leaned against the counter with her back to the open living area. She—no, they—should have known better.

"Yes, Son, I was."

"Oh. Does this mean Renee will be my new mommy?"

Aaron glanced back and grasped her hand. "Too soon to say. Daddies and possible new mommies have to spend time together before they know if God wants them to get married."

"Good answer, Son."

Renee spun around. Standing in the living room, looking right in the kitchen, were Aaron's parents. Renee prayed the floor would open up and swallow her whole. How could she have not heard Aaron's parents come in through the front door?

Aaron coughed and cleared his throat. "Hi, Mom, Dad."

His father spoke first. "I guess we stopped in at the wrong time."

Aaron placed his arm around Renee's shoulders. "We're heading out to the zoo for the day. Would you folks like to join us?" he offered.

His mother answered in Spanish. Renee couldn't speak. She couldn't look at his parents or Adam. She felt too guilty. *Why? You've been wanting to kiss him. Obviously he's been wanting to kiss you too. It's one thing being caught by Adam, but by his parents. . .* She felt the heat on her cheeks increase enough that a cool compress sounded desirable. Of course, with the amount of heat she was feeling, steam would probably rise from the cloth.

"Speak in English, Mom. Renee doesn't understand."

*"Si.* Yes. Sorry. I was apologizing for walking in," Gladys Chapin explained to Renee.

Embarrassment flooded her cheeks. Renee realized she wasn't being condemned. And it wasn't her place to say whether or not it was a problem. Obviously they had a key and were used to just walking in. Which would be perfectly natural with Gladys taking care of Adam.

"Mother, relax, no harm done."

Adam went to his grandmother and hugged her.

"Excuse me." Renee stepped from Aaron's embrace and left to finish clearing the table. She needed to do something, anything. How could she have allowed herself to get carried away like that? Or Aaron, for that matter?

He came up behind her. "Renee," he whispered.

She jumped and turned to face him.

"I won't apologize for kissing you, but I am sorry that we didn't pick a more appropriate time. Next time, I'll be more careful."

"Aaron, I'm so embarrassed."

"Shh." He pulled her back into his embrace. "Don't fret about it. My parents were well aware of my growing affections toward you."

"But. . ."

"Shh." He placed his finger to her lips. "It was an awkward

moment, but we'll survive. Come on, the zoo awaits."

Renee picked up the box of donuts and handed it to him. The rest of the items she removed.

"Are you folks going to join us?" Aaron asked upon re-entering the kitchen.

"No, Son. One of the reasons we came over was Marie."

Aaron stiffened. "Is she all right?"

"Yes, Manuel's disappeared again. I figure he came into some money somehow and is drinking it away." Charles sighed. "Your mother and I thought it would be good to visit Marie and the children."

"I'll pray for you and your visit." Aaron placed the box of donuts on the counter.

"Thank you." Charles turned toward Renee. "It was nice to see you, Renee. Perhaps you can get this guy to invite you over to the family meal tomorrow after church."

Renee cleared her throat. "Food?" She wiggled her eyebrows. The room erupted in laughter.

"Grandma, Renee can eat a whole pizza," Adam boasted.

"She can? My, my." Gladys giggled. "Where does she keep it? She's too skinny."

It was true, she was skinny, always had been, despite eating like a horse. It had made so many of her roommates in college jealous of her eating habits.

Aaron lifted his hands in surrender. "You invited that one on yourself, Girl."

"I run," she defended.

❧

Aaron put the dollar in the machine that would make a plastic model of three monkeys. He remembered having his own set of zoo creatures when he was a child. He chuckled. They hadn't improved on the machine. It still worked the same, smelled the same. Memories washed over him to a time when he and Marie were both small and didn't have a care in the world.

"Penny for your thoughts," Renee whispered.

Aaron turned. "Where's Adam?"

"On the slide. It's great that they put these play areas in for the children."

"Yeah, gives the parents a chance to catch their wind. Why can't we bundle that energy? We'd make a fortune."

Renee chuckled.

The large spatula pushed the newly formed plastic monkeys down to the bin waiting below.

She scrunched her nose. "It's a noisy thing."

"Did you put sunblock on your nose?"

"Yes, why?" She placed her delicate fingers on the top ridge of her nose.

"It's turning pink."

"Oh no." She ran to her backpack and ruffled through for the sunblock.

"I burn easily," she mumbled.

"I figured." Aaron sat on the bench and watched Adam for a moment. "Here, let me reapply it to your shoulders and back."

She handed him the bottle, then lifted her ponytail.

He pressed his finger against her pink skin and saw the white imprint. "You might already be burnt."

"Ugh," she groaned. "I probably should have worn a blouse with short sleeves and a high neckline."

"You look just fine, but you probably would have been better prepared for the sun. I've heard people with fair skin really have to be careful. You ought to wear a hat too."

"Yeah, right and look like a tourist. I don't think so," she quipped.

"Oh, so sun poisoning is a better alternative?"

"I'm not that badly burnt, am I?"

"I don't think so, but like I said, I'm not used to such fair skin."

"Where's the nearest rest room? I'd better go check."

Aaron pointed it out on the map. "Adam and I will wait right here for you."

"Okay." She bolted off. He'd never seen her run. Her form

was excellent. *Had she competed in college?* he wondered.

"Daddy," Adam squealed as he slid down the slide.

"Hey, Buddy, having fun?"

"A blast."

Aaron's cell phone rang. "Hello."

"Mr. Chapin, this is Detective Diaz."

Aaron rolled his eyes and leaned his head back. "Yes, Detective?" Why'd he ever given the man his cell phone number?

"Your store's been vandalized."

"What?"

"It doesn't appear that anything is missing, but someone threw a huge hunk of coral through the front door. I'm afraid I need you to come to your office to verify that nothing was stolen."

"I'm in South Miami at the Metro Zoo. It'll take me an hour to get there."

"No problem. I'll have an officer stand guard until you come."

"Thanks."

"Adam," Aaron called. "We've got to go, Son."

"But why, Daddy? We haven't seen the zebras yet."

"Next time, Sport. Someone threw a rock through the office door. I have to take care of it."

"Why would someone throw a rock, Daddy? Didn't their mommy and daddy tell them not to throw rocks?"

"I guess they weren't listening to their parents."

"They need to get a spanking and be sent to their rooms, huh, Daddy?"

Aaron scooped up his son and held him close to his chest. *Lord, help me protect Adam from the truth. And what is the truth, Lord? Why am I being targeted? No other storefronts have been recent victims. At least not that I'm aware of.*

Aaron straddled Renee's backpack over his left shoulder and left the play area to walk in the direction she'd been going. "Look for Renee, Buddy."

"Okay."

"Ugh," he grunted, wincing from Adam using his hair as an anchor. "Son, would you mind leaving my hair on my head?"

"Sorry, Daddy.

"I see her," Adam shouted, bouncing up and down. Which was worse—ribs kicked or hair pulled—Aaron wasn't sure. He bent down and let the offending feet hurry off to their target.

Renee opened her arms wide and cradled the boy as he slammed into her with full force. Aaron grinned.

Her eyes locked with his. Aaron nodded. Obviously Adam had shared the news.

"Can I drop you off with Adam at my place while I deal with the police?"

"Sure. I'll make supper. Leave me Adam's car seat, and we'll go grocery shopping if I can't find what I need."

"And she cooks," he chuckled.

# eleven

"You better believe it, Buster," Renee snapped. "I had to in order to survive."

"Huh?"

*Oh dear, I've said too much. . .think, quick!* "Remember I told you my aunt wasn't much of a parent figure?"

Aaron nodded.

"Well, she didn't cook. And you know how much I like food."

"Junk food," he corrected. Pulling out his keys, he handed her the backpack. "Hop in, Sport."

Aaron opened the door for Renee. *A gentleman.* She melted into the front seat.

"Buckle up, Adam."

Renee heard the click of the buckle latching. "Did you have fun, Adam?"

"Yeah. I liked the giraffes. They have really long necks."

Renee thought back on how far they had to spread their front legs in order to bend down far enough for them to eat the grass.

Aaron slipped behind the wheel.

"What about how slow that tortoise moved?" Aaron asked as he turned the key in the ignition.

"The gorilla scared me."

"Me too," Renee agreed. "I thought he was going to come through the viewing window."

"He picked his nose, Daddy. It was gross."

"Eww," Aaron and Renee said in unison.

They spoke for awhile about the various sights and sounds of the zoo. In spite of the wonderful day, her mind kept jumping to the office. Who had broken the door? Was it another robbery attempt?

Aaron reached over and took her hand. "I'm sorry about this."

"Phooey, you didn't break the door." She glanced back. Adam was nodding off to sleep. "Do you think it's the same person as before?"

"I don't know. I guess I just assumed it was, but more than likely it was kids with nothing better to do."

"True. The last time it was at night, and they were professional. This time, well, we don't know yet, but it seems like it's possible the two are unrelated."

"Quite." Aaron glanced over at her. "So, what are you fixing for dinner?"

"You'll just have to be pleasantly surprised."

"Hmm, well you know how I like my steak," he rambled. "I had a wonderful time today, Renee. Thanks for coming."

"I wouldn't have missed it."

He lifted her hand and kissed it. "I'd like to take you out on a real date, just the two of us. What do you think?"

Was she ready to go to the next level in the relationship?

"Renee?"

"I'm sorry, I guess I'm still afraid."

"I thought we settled that last week."

"We discussed it. Sometimes deciding something isn't the same as acting on it."

"Okay, I'll give you that. Let's pray about it; does that sound reasonable to you?"

"Aaron, you're unlike anyone I've ever known. I love that you want to pray about everything, but I'm also taken aback by it. Do you pray before you decide on all matters?"

Aaron let out a guttural sigh. "No, I'm not perfect. I'd love to say I always act in a spiritual manner and put the Lord first in everything, but I fail miserably at times. I do want the Lord to be central in our relationship. I don't want to have Adam's expectations high when it's possible nothing more will develop other than a mutual friendship."

"Has he been asking for a new mother for awhile?"

Aaron released her hand and placed both hands back on the steering wheel. He leaned back in his bucket seat and nodded his head. "For a few weeks now. Honestly, when he first approached me about the idea, I couldn't see past the loss of Hannah. Now, well now, I think it's possible. But I want to be cautious. There's no question about the attraction between us, and I truly enjoy our conversation but. . ."

"But are we good for one another?"

He glanced over at her and smiled, then broke the connection and concentrated on the highway. "I don't have time to waste on dating anyone who comes my way. I'm just not interested in frittering away my time on such relationships. I do believe the Lord is bringing us together, but the questions remain."

Accepting the possibility that this attraction to Aaron could come from the Lord had kept her tossing and turning more than one night. "Aaron, I don't want to repeat my past mistakes. Brent used me. I know that now. But I used him. I wanted a husband. I felt I needed one to be complete. I've been working on trying to be complete in who I am with the Lord and understanding that I don't need a man for that."

"You're right. You don't need a man to be complete."

"I also have a past that's been colored by my environment. I'm concerned that I didn't have a good role model, at least one I can remember, on how to have a good relationship with the opposite sex. I thought I'd been a good partner with Brent, but apparently I was fooling myself. There's so much you don't know about me and—"

He covered her hand with his again. "Shh, that's why I want to spend time with you. Let's take this to the next level and see."

"I'm just afraid."

"Honey, I know you're afraid, and I'll try not to hurt you. But if we put God as the center, He'll make it clear whether we should go forward or if we should simply shake hands and be friends."

Did she trust God? Could she trust God with her heart? "All

right, I'll try to step out in faith and trust the Lord knows what He's doing. Because truthfully, I promised myself I would never fall in love with another boss."

"I can remedy that."

"How?"

"You're fired." He wiggled his eyebrows and flashed a white toothy grin.

"You can't be serious," she protested.

"Of course not. But if that's what it takes, I'm attracted enough to you that I'm willing to risk losing the best employee I've ever had in order to date her and explore the possibilities of another partnership."

"You're that confident?"

"Renee, I'm not looking for a business partner. There are tons of people who could do your job. Probably not as exceptionally as you can, but there are others out there. What's developing between us is worth far more than any business. I'd risk it all, if I was certain you were the one."

"But you don't know me."

He paused at that.

*What is he thinking?*

"Look, I know you have things in your past. I have things or events in my past you don't know about either. You don't know how I fell in love with Hannah, how she meant so much to me that she was a part of the very air I breathed."

"Could you love someone like that again?" she asked.

"Honestly, I don't know. I suppose it would be a different love because we are different people. But I swear to you, I would never enter a relationship in which I didn't feel God making us into a threefold cord."

"Threefold cord?"

"Ecclesiastes 4:12. Solomon writes that a threefold cord is not easily broken. One cord made of three parts."

"Ah." *How can I argue against Scripture?* She'd never met a man with his head so straight about the Word, life, love. It was a wee bit scary. "Are you like some sort of superhuman, spiritually topnotch kind of icon?"

Aaron laughed. "Once you get to know me better, you'll start finding my faults. But it's nice to know I don't have any at the moment." He winked.

"Hmm," she mumbled and looked ahead to the oncoming traffic. They'd be at his house in a couple minutes. "Aaron, why don't you take my car to the office, and we can let Adam rest for a moment or two longer in yours."

"You don't mind?"

"Nope. I like my car, but I'm not overly attached to it."

"Woman, you scare me. That's a classic in prime condition."

"I bought it secondhand, possibly thirdhand, when I was a kid. I gradually had the work done on it. It was a real bomb when I first got it. Which is why I could afford it. Brent paid me well—that's one good thing I can say on Brent's behalf. As you can see by my apartment, I keep a simple life. Computers and gadgets are my biggest weakness. I don't know if you saw my system."

"I noticed. Okay, I'll take your car, and I'll be back as soon as possible." He pulled into the parking space next to her car and turned off the engine.

She handed him the keys.

"I'll call you when I know what's up. Take my cell phone." He unclipped his phone from his belt and handed it to her.

A pregnant pause passed. Did he not want to leave as much as she didn't want him to leave? They were just beginning to open up to each other. Could she be patient and allow the Lord to work here? "Be careful."

"I will."

He leaned closer. Was he going to kiss her again? Did she want him to? *Ha, no question.* Her skin tingled in anticipation. He cupped her chin in his palm.

She reached out and traced his lips.

He rested his forehead on hers and slipped his hand behind her neck. "Father," he whispered. "Help us stay focused on You and not our own desires."

The tension broken, he kissed her gently on the lips. "I'll be back as soon as possible."

Before she opened her eyes, he was getting out of the car and into hers, murmuring, "Lord, give me strength."

Stunned and uncertain if she was pleased with his prayer, she leaned back in the bucket seat and looked toward the white wisps of clouds spun like cotton candy. *Who is this man, Lord? I've respected him in the way he's conducted his business. But he'd never seemed overly Christian. Am I less of a Christian? Have I messed up that part of my life too?* She had remembered the verse he quoted once he said where it came from, but. . .

*I feel like a beginner next to him. Lord, something's wrong here. You can't possibly think that I have anything to offer him to make him complete.*

Then it hit her. Aaron was complete without her. Just as she was complete without him. The cord was something God created when He united two people. It wasn't something lacking in her or in Aaron, or Brent, for that matter. *Why have I believed for so long that a man would complete me?*

*Because your aunt did and tried on every man she could find.*

Renee nibbled her lower lip. *Lord, help me trust You, not myself.*

"Renee, why are you crying?" Adam asked.

❧

Arriving at the office, Aaron found a minor mess. Nothing missing, nothing disturbed. Even Detective Diaz had left word at the scene that he felt the two events were unrelated. Aaron called a glass company that said they could have someone there in an hour. He dialed his home phone number. No answer.

He dialed his cell. Adam answered. "Hi, Dad."

"How's it going, Buddy?"

"Good. We're shopping."

"Oh, what's Renee buying?"

Adam giggled. "She said I couldn't say. It's a secret."

"Oh. Can I talk to Renee?"

"Okay. Renee," Adam yelled. Aaron pulled the phone from his ear.

"Tried to get it out of him, huh?" she teased.

"Can't blame a man for trying. I'm stuck here for two hours, I think. The glass man said he'd send someone here in an hour."

"No problem. Adam and I are having a good time. And he's telling me all your secrets."

"Oh, and what secrets are those?"

"Something about how I shouldn't open up any of your closets because I might not be able to get the doors shut."

Aaron groaned. "Hey, I never said I was a good house-keeper. Mom comes by every few months and takes care of some of my cleaning."

"You don't pay that woman enough."

"I know. I don't know what I'd do without her. I'll let you get back to your shopping. I should be home around five. I'll call if it's going to take longer."

"Bye, Aaron."

"Bye." He hung up the phone. "What could she possibly be making?"

❧

Over the next few weeks Aaron discovered that Renee definitely could cook. From Italian to stir-fry, he hadn't sampled anything that didn't please his palate. They'd also gone out a time or two alone and several times with Adam. Work had kept them busy, but with fewer and fewer sales. Even his attempts to approach new customers had failed. Someone else consistently beat him to them. How could one area of his life be going so well and another area be failing so miserably? It was almost like someone was reading his mind.

The initial contact with the FBI seemed pointless. Even Detective Diaz had uncovered nothing. All that equipment and not one item showing up in a pawnshop.

Aaron came into his office and found John working at his new drafting table. "Hey, John. Where's Renee?"

"She said to tell you she was picking up Adam and that they had a surprise for you."

"A surprise, huh?" Memories of the first surprise meal still warmed his belly.

"You two are getting pretty thick. Anything serious?" John put down his pencil.

"Too soon to tell. We're just taking it one step at a time."

"Yeah, right. One minute you're just working together, the next you're thick as thieves."

Aaron chuckled. "Maybe so."

The computer hummed to life with a few keystrokes. "John, did you use my computer to upload today?"

"Nope, haven't touched it. What's up?" John straightened on his stool.

"Nothing, I guess. Renee must have used it." *But that doesn't make sense since she has everything on her system.* Aaron scratched the day's growth on his jaw.

"What on earth?"

"What's the matter?" John came up beside him.

"My passwords aren't working."

"Did you type them in wrong?"

It was a dumb thing to say, and he knew the kid meant well but. . . "Yes." He tried again. No response.

The phone rang.

"Sunny Flo Designs, Aaron speaking."

Click. The receiver went dead.

"Try your passwords, John."

John leaned over and typed in his code. He had access—limited, but still he had access.

"Try Renee's," John suggested.

Aaron typed in Renee's codes. He entered and had total access. But what he found on the site was a folder he'd never seen before. He clicked it open and collapsed in his chair.

"No way," John objected.

# twelve

"Are we really going to fry a whole turkey?" Adam asked.

"Yup." Renee loaded another gallon of peanut oil into her trunk.

"Cool."

Thanksgiving was a few days away, and together she and Adam had been planning a surprise for the holiday. A traditional family Thanksgiving lodged somewhere in the back of her mind. She remembered being six and visiting with all the relatives, everyone laughing, the house loud, and so much food. Plans with Gladys and Charles Chapin would help to make this a special Thanksgiving for Aaron and Adam.

"Okay, let's get these things to my apartment before your daddy figures out what we're doing."

"I like surprises."

She raked her fingers through his curls. "Me too."

Adam secured himself in his booster seat, and she crossed herself with the seat belt.

"Can we put the top down?" he asked.

"Sure." Renee unbuckled her seat belt and unhooked the top's latches. She turned on the power. Adam swiveled back and forth, watching the end unfold and the roof go higher. She opened the trunk and pulled out the leather saddle that covered the collapsed top. Putting the roof down took some work, but for Adam's pleasure, why not?

Her new cell phone rang. Aaron hadn't needed to twist her arm too much to purchase one. "Adam, could you answer that for me?"

"Okay. Hello?"

Renee snapped the last snap into place.

"Hi, Daddy."

She slipped behind the steering wheel and held off starting up the car.

Adam nodded his head.

"Say yes, Adam. He can't see you shaking your head."

"Yes," he replied and smiled. "Okay." He handed her the phone. "Daddy wants to talk to you."

"Thanks, Buddy." She slipped the phone up to her ear. "Hi, Aaron, what's up?"

"Renee, did you change my passwords today?"

*A little testy, are we?* "No, what's wrong?"

"My passwords aren't working. Yours and John's are, but mine aren't."

"That's weird. Are you sure you typed—"

"Yes, I tried and retried it several times. Renee, that's not all. There's a file in your secure area," he stammered. "Ah, well, it appears as. . ."

"What are you trying to say, Aaron?"

"I think you'd better come here and see for yourself. It's rather hard to explain."

Renee nibbled her lower lip. It didn't sound good, whatever it was. "Sure, I've got to run to my apartment first so some food doesn't spoil, but I'll be there shortly, okay?"

"Good, and Renee, for what it's worth, I trust you."

"Thanks." *I think.* She glanced in her rearview mirror. A man stood across the street staring at her. A chill wrapped its icy fingers around her spine. She looked again. He was gone. Her mind was playing tricks on her. *Get a grip,* she reprimanded herself.

"Change of plans, Buddy. We'll drop off the turkey at my house, then head over to the office. Your dad needs me to look at something." Slowly, she backed the car out of its parking space, still looking for the stranger. Maybe she shouldn't have watched that gangster movie last night.

"Okay." Adam wiggled his feet, covered with tennis shoes.

The wind whipped Renee's hair. She grabbed a scrunchy and pulled it back at the next stoplight.

"I like the wind." Adam beamed.

"Me too." Dreams of traveling the shoreline with no other cars on the road, the wind, the sun, the sandy beaches, filled her mind. *Get real. This is Miami.* Skyscrapers and tourist-filled streets—she wouldn't be putting the pedal to the metal here. *Ah, but one can dream,* she mused. A gentle smile erased the tension she'd been feeling since Aaron's call.

A few minutes later she was in the basement garage of her apartment building. "Okay, Buddy, let's get this turkey in the refrigerator." Renee sorted through the various bags, taking out the food items that needed refrigeration. The rest could stay in the trunk.

"What can I carry?"

A grin swept over her face. "Here ya go."

"Renee?"

"Yes, Adam?" They walked toward the elevator.

"Do you like my daddy?"

*Uh-oh, where was this going?* She gave a tentative, "Yes."

Adam nodded his head. She pushed the up button. He held the plastic bag with two hands. "Do you want to be a mommy?"

*Swoosh.* The elevator doors opened. "Uh, yes, someday," she stammered.

They stepped inside. She pushed the button to her floor.

"Grandma says mommies and daddies have to marry before they have children."

Renee nodded her head. She looked down at him. His eyebrows were knit together, his lower lip puckered slightly. Something was really troubling the poor boy. The doors opened. "Come on, Buddy."

He followed, carrying his load.

She placed her key in the lock and turned it.

"Renee?"

"Yes, Buddy?" Perhaps he was ready now to ask his question.

She opened the door. One look inside and she dropped the turkey, pushed Adam back, grabbed him, and ran.

Aaron flew out of the office, stopped, and ran back in. "John, lock up for me."

"Sure."

John opened his mouth to continue but didn't have time. "Later, John." Aaron rushed through the door again.

"God, keep them safe," he prayed, jumping into his van and heading toward his parents' house. Renee had called saying she was taking Adam to his grandparents and that Aaron needed to be there as soon as she arrived.

The fear in her voice and the short message, "I can't talk now," brought instant adrenaline to his veins. "What's going on, Lord? First I find the bogus file, now this. What's happening?"

He wormed his way through the city's back streets. Rush hour and highways were not a good combination in Miami. He'd make better time with the stoplights of the residential sections.

The classic blue Mustang in his parents' drive gave him a smidgen of relief. He skidded up to the curb and cut the engine before coming to a complete stop. He leaped out of the car and took the front lawn in five long strides. "Adam, Renee," he hollered as he ran through the front door.

His mother's worried face nodded they were in the kitchen.

"Daddy." Adam came running into his arms. "Renee saved me from a bad man."

"What?" Adam held his son closer.

"She ran real fast. And we didn't take the elevator. She ran down the stairs so fast. We. . .we. . ."

"Slow down, Sport. Where was the bad man?"

"In her apartment."

"Who is this bad man?"

"I don't know. I didn't see him. Renee just told me that's why we were running. She's still on the phone with the police."

He needed to speak with Renee, but it was essential to calm Adam. He appeared to be settling down. *But. . .* "Are you okay?"

"Yeah, I was scared at first. She held me tight. I didn't put on my seat belt right away. Renee said I could do it while we drove."

*Who was in her apartment?* Aaron stepped toward the kitchen and heard Renee's mumbled words from the back patio.

"Adam, will you stay with Grandma while I talk to Renee?"

"Okay." Adam hugged him hard. "I love you, Daddy."

"I love you too." Adam slid down. Aaron watched him go to his grandmother. *Thank You, Lord. You protected him.*

He stepped onto the patio where Renee paced back and forth. She held up her hand to him, then spoke impatiently into the phone. "I'm telling you, he was there."

She walked farther away. "Then arrest me. Look." She let out an exasperated sigh. "I know what I saw. Why would I call you if I hadn't?"

She turned back toward Aaron and rolled her eyes in apparent frustration.

"Give me a break. Look, remember that sealed file you came across?"

*Sealed file. What is she talking about?* Aaron wondered.

"It has to have something to do with that case. No, I don't want to tell you what it's all about."

Renee stood still. "All right." He watched her close her eyes, then open them slowly. *She's shutting down her emotions.*

"Good-bye."

She closed the phone and stared blankly in front of her.

He eased forward a step.

She turned to face him. "Aaron, I can't tell you what's happened."

"No way, Renee. You owe me some kind of explanation."

"All right, my past has caught up with me. I don't know how, and I don't know why, but I need to disappear for awhile."

"You what? You've got to be kidding. You're acting like some kind of a spy or something." He calmed himself. "Renee, we mean too much to each other. Don't do this. Talk to me."

Her shoulders relaxed. Tears glistened in her eyes.

"I'd love to, but I can't. Not now; there isn't time. You'll have to trust me on this."

"Who's after you, Renee, and why?"

"I can't, Aaron. I can't put you and Adam at risk. You mean too much to me."

"This is crazy. You have to trust someone. Trust me." He pulled her into his arms and held her tight.

She circled her arms around him and shivered in his embrace. For a long moment she stayed in his arms. Finding her strength, she pushed away.

"I'll call you when I'm safe." She bolted from the patio and ran through the kitchen.

"No way," he roared and ran after her.

❧

*How'd he find me, Lord? After all these years; two different states, and still he finds me. How?*

Renee heard Aaron calling out to her. She had to leave. She had to protect him and Adam.

"Renee," Aaron yelled. "You can't leave like this."

She squeezed her eyes shut. Looking back would give her pause, and if she paused, her heart would win over her mind. Logically, she knew what she had to do. In the early years she had prepared for her escape if ever the need arose. But as time went by, she'd almost forgotten.

Almost.

Fumbling with the keys, she jammed the ignition key in place.

"Renee, stop! Please stop. I love you. Don't leave me like this."

Her hands shook; the tears freely fell. "Aaron, it's because I love you. I have to leave."

"Whatever it is, the Lord will see us through this."

She leaned her forehead against the steering wheel.

"Please, Renee, stop long enough to tell me."

He opened the door and placed a loving hand on her back.

"Please, trust me, Renee."

She looked up at the blurred image of the man she loved. He knelt beside her and placed his left hand on her knee.

"Talk to me. What could you possibly have done that I wouldn't forgive you?"

"It's not that; it's who he is. He doesn't forgive. He's the epitome of hatred."

"Who?"

"He must have gotten out on good behavior or something. He was supposed to be in prison for twenty years."

He rubbed her back gently and waited.

Should she tell him? If he knew, would he be in danger? *To spite me, he'd come after Adam and Aaron.* She shook her head no. "I'm sorry, Aaron, I can't put your lives in danger."

"Why can't you tell the police?"

She wiped the tears from her eyes.

"I don't know. I guess because Detective Diaz still believes I'm behind the break-in at the office. Do you know what he found in my apartment?"

Aaron shook his head no.

"The old computer. Your old computer. Can you believe that? If I was going to rob the place, do you think I'd want the old computer? It's such a dinosaur."

She shook off the train of thought. "The fact is, Diaz doesn't believe me that. . .he. . .was in the apartment. He said I was just trying to cloud the investigation. And what's this about a file of E-mails?"

"There's a hidden file on the server that came up when we logged in as you. It contains E-mails between you and another company, B&J Advertising. You were offering my database of clients for a fee."

"You can't believe I did that."

"Of course not. It's too obvious. Even if you were at fault, you wouldn't have kept a record that I could have stumbled upon. Personally, I think someone is trying to set you up."

"Trying," she huffed. "I'd say Diaz is certain of it."

"Don't be too sure. He plays the devil's advocate for certain, but I think he believes you."

"I don't know what to do, Aaron. You don't know the man like I do, and I couldn't live with myself if something were to happen to you or Adam."

"Trust God, Renee. All along our relationship has been slowly developing with God at the center. Just because something horrible from the past has come to haunt you, don't stop trusting the Lord."

"But—"

He held his finger to her lips.

"Honey, whoever this guy is has found out where you live. He probably already knows where you work and who you work for."

"True, Benny would do a thorough investigation."

"Benny who?"

*Oh, no.* "I'm sorry, I didn't mean to say anything."

He caressed her jaw with the feather touch of his finger.

"Did he rape you?" He ached for her, his chocolate eyes so expressive.

"No, nothing like that. He lived with my aunt on a fairly regular basis for a time. He drank, and when he drank he'd beat her. I came home once when he was beating her. And well, I tried to yell at him to stop. He didn't. He landed a solid blow to my jaw. I grabbed the closest thing handy, my baseball bat."

Aaron's eyes widened.

"I'd just come home from softball practice. Anyway, I swung and connected. I broke his arm. He managed to get the bat from me and hit me again. By the time the police came, the bruises were showing. Not to mention my cracked rib. He had me arrested. My aunt wouldn't back up my story. She was terrified that he'd be released and come and beat her again, I guess. Anyway, in a nutshell, that's what happened and why I have a sealed record. Connecticut has changed the laws recently, extending the time for sealed records to be on file. Detective Diaz wouldn't have found it if the old law still applied. Benny was a small-time dealer and thug for hire. The cop arrested him too and was happy to get him off the streets. And since I was a minor, he received a greater sentence, and the charges against me were dropped.

"I don't trust him," Renee continued, "and I can't have him hurt you or Adam. He's like that, Aaron. He's spiteful beyond compare. If he knows I care for anyone, he'd go after that person first, then me. Or worse yet, he'd make me watch."

"Come here." Aaron directed. She leaned toward him, and he wrapped her in his protective arms. "Father, we come before You and hand this situation with Benny over to You. Keep Renee safe from harm. Keep all of us safe. Show us what to do and how to handle it."

Renee cleared her throat. "And, Lord, help me with my lack of faith. Help me to trust You completely with everything in my life. And thank You for Aaron." He squeezed her hand. "In Jesus' name, amen."

"Amen."

The truth was out, and Aaron didn't think her horrible. She probably should have told him ages ago. "Oh, no."

"What?" He turned the engine off.

"Where am I going to live?"

# thirteen

Aaron slipped her keys into his pocket. "Okay, let's take this one step at a time. First, we need to go to your apartment and see if Benny's still there or if he left a message for you. Second, I also need your help in tracking those phony E-mails, how they got on our server."

"I don't know, Aaron. I think you're better off without me. Do you think Benny could be behind all the problems at the office?" Fear centered in her eyes.

"Is Benny good with computers?"

"Not that I know of. He could have learned in prison, I suppose."

"True. Come." He took her hand and encouraged her out of the driver's seat. "Let's go back in the house and talk things through."

"But your parents? Do they know?"

"About the business? Some. About the detective's suspicions regarding you, no."

"Oh." She looked down at her feet.

He lifted her chin with his index finger, willing her to look at him. "Renee, you were the victim. Why are you afraid to let people know what happened?"

"I spent nearly a year in custody. Rumors got out, and when I returned to school, no one wanted to be around me. We were living in an apartment building, and several classmates saw me carted off in handcuffs."

He held her close. *Help me reassure her, Lord.* "But Honey, that was years ago. Today people know you for who you are, not what you did. Besides, it seems to me, it was self-defense."

"Some defense. He beat me bad. The worst betrayal was from my aunt. She lied to the police. Well, she didn't exactly lie. She just refused to speak and wouldn't agree with my account of the incident. Benny supported her habit at the time. I guess she didn't want to lose that."

*Benny seems like a real gem, Lord. How can she fight this monster?* "Renee, we'll need to fill my mother in for Adam's sake, if nothing else. She's seen you upset. Can't you tell her why?"

"I don't want to put her in harm's way, Aaron." She pulled out of his arms. "I really should go away."

He grabbed her hand. "No, we'll fight this together. I'm not your aunt, Renee. I'll stand by you. You forget, I've dealt with a man who beats on women. I know how to stand up to these guys."

Aaron escorted her back to the front door. Adam would be safe here, he hoped and prayed. They went inside and, after Renee filled his mother in, she offered Renee a place to stay. Aaron had never been more proud of his mother, of her generous spirit, and he knew she would accept Renee as part of the family. The phrase "part of the family" continued to play in his mind as they drove toward Renee's apartment.

"Aaron, are you okay?" Renee's gentle touch brought him from his musings.

"I'm fine. Sorry." He noted the speed and pushed the accelerator. He glanced over. "Honey, it'll be all right. I doubt he's still around. And if he is, all the better. I'll be able to confront him."

She nodded.

His cell phone rang. "Hello."

"Mr. Chapin, it's Detective Diaz."

"Yes, Detective." Aaron sighed.

Renee whipped her head toward him.

"Have you heard from Renee Austin?"

"Yes, she's with me now."

"Did she tell you what we found in her apartment?"

"Yes."

"There's more."

"What?" Aaron captured her hand and squeezed it slightly.

"Those E-mails came from that computer."

Aaron glanced at the rearview mirror. "Is that really a surprise? Someone's setting her up."

"Appears that way, but you know I can't overlook the obvious."

"Yeah, yeah."

Aaron slowed down as the flow of traffic stopped for the tollbooth. "Hang on a minute." He cupped the phone. "Do you want to tell him about Benny? I think you should."

She shook her head no.

"All right."

"Is there anything else, Detective?"

"We're working on those E-mails. I've contacted the company where they came from. No one at the company goes by that name."

"I'm not surprised."

"No, I suppose that would have been too easy. Here's my problem: They were sent from that company too. Whoever this is had to have access to this company's E-mail service and set up a dummy E-mail address. Seems to me someone is going to a tremendous amount of trouble just to try and frame Ms. Austin. But here's where it gets interesting. This frame is superficial; it would never hold up in court. Let me ask you why, Mr. Chapin? Why would someone go to all that trouble?"

"I honestly couldn't tell you."

"Also, the feds would like to speak with you about a possible sting operation."

"Great. When?"

❧

Renee tried not to listen to Aaron's conversation, but she was sitting right beside him. *Why can't I tell Detective Diaz? Am I so vain?* She worried her lower lip.

She'd never been more thankful in her life than when her aunt decided to move to New York. Her senior year in high school had brought welcomed relief. No one knew about her past, and she refused to tell anyone.

Aaron pulled up to the parking garage. She pushed her remote and the gate opened. *How did Benny get in here? Security oozes from every corner.* At least she thought it did. Now that was up for debate.

He pulled into her numbered parking spot.

It seemed an eternity ago that she'd been in here with Adam, joyfully bringing up some of the food for their Thanksgiving feast.

Aaron continued his call as they headed for the elevator.

The super, dressed in his gray work clothes, called over to her. "Evening, Ms. Austin. Did you see your father?"

"Father?"

"Yeah, I let him into your apartment earlier. He said he wanted to surprise you."

"He's not my father. My father died when I was eight." She held back the scream.

A pallor washed over the middle-aged super. "Oh dear. I'm so sorry."

"Excuse me," Aaron interrupted, clicking his cell phone shut. "You let a stranger into her apartment?"

"I'm sorry. He seemed. . ." The man stammered.

"It's all right," Renee interjected. "But in the future, no one, absolutely no one, can come to my apartment without my permission. All right?"

"Yes, Ms. Austin. It won't happen again."

"Thank you."

Aaron held her in a protective embrace. "Well that settles how he got in."

"Yeah," she mumbled. "But what about the computer? How'd that get in there? Did Benny let the guy put it in? Or was it already in there when Benny arrived? In that case, someone besides the super has access to my apartment. Either way, I'll have to stay with your parents until the locks are changed."

"You're right."

"What was all that other stuff you and the detective were talking about?"

"I can't tell you. I want to, but they asked me not to because—"

"Because I'm still a suspect."

Aaron nodded his head.

Would she ever be free of the past? Should she tell Diaz and get it over with? It's not like other people haven't been tried and convicted for crimes they didn't commit. *I was innocent, but I still had to go to counseling.* The stigma of having been beaten, arrested, and put away still tore at her heart. *Will I ever be free, Lord?*

Aaron pulled her keys out from his pocket. "Which one?" he asked.

"This one." She pointed to the silver key with a blue plastic ring around the end. She'd identified it for quick and easy recognition. Not that it mattered much if anyone could get past the super. She might very well need to look into moving.

Placing the key in the lock, Aaron opened the door. "Stay here while I check the place."

Renee nodded. Her heart started to race. Why did she let him talk her into coming back here? She could have just bought new clothes. Although she'd want to get her computer, if it was still there. Would Benny steal it?

"All clear, Renee. Come in." Aaron held the door open. Slowly, she entered.

The apartment seemed different somehow. Nothing was out of place, but the invasion hung in the air like a thick fog over the harbor in the fall.

Aaron rubbed her shoulders. "It's all right, Renee. I'm here."

"Did the police take the old computer?"

"Yes."

"Great."

"It's circumstantial, Renee. Plus Diaz has been in your apartment. He knows it wasn't here before."

She sighed. "I'm going to have to tell him, aren't I?"

"It would be helpful for him, but it isn't necessary. I understand you're wanting to keep it hidden, but. . ." He paused and turned her to face him. "I think it would be easier if you did tell him. It's not your fault, Renee. It was self-defense."

"It's not shame; it's fear. I was arrested and held for so long. If I hadn't had a Christian caseworker, I think I would have gone crazy."

He smiled.

"What?"

"I was wondering where God was during that time. You just said He was there looking out for you, in spite of your circumstances. It's reassuring to hear."

"Oh, well, I suppose you're right. I attended her church for awhile. Then we moved to New York."

"Where's your aunt now?"

"I have no idea. When I went to college, I came home and discovered she'd moved out. I never heard from her again."

"Not once?"

"Nope. She hated my going to church. I guess it reminded her of everything she gave up when she left Uncle Pete. He remarried, and that really bothered her. You know, it's strange, but why is it that the ones who do the sinning blame everyone else for their problems? Aunt Ida always blamed Uncle Pete, but she was the one who left him."

"When we're sinning, we like to pass the buck. That way we don't have to acknowledge our sin. Look at my sister Marie. She still won't leave Manuel, who, by the way, has been back for a week."

The red glow of her answering machine blinked. She hit the play button.

Aaron opened the refrigerator and took out a bottle of water. She'd started keeping them in the house ever since they'd started dating.

The first message let her know that her dry cleaning was done.

The second came from John. "Hey, Renee, if ya see the boss,

tell him the McPherson account called and gave the go-ahead."

Renee smiled.

"Thank You, Lord." Aaron saluted toward the ceiling with his bottled water in hand.

They'd worked long and hard on that proposal and had kept it completely between the two of them. She turned toward Aaron. "Finally," she sighed.

"Yes, and we can prove you aren't the leak."

"Maybe. Diaz will probably say I let the sale go through to keep the attention off of myself."

Aaron shook his head. "You don't trust the police, do you?"

"No." She pushed the play button to continue her messages.

"Well, well, if it isn't my old friend. Hello, Renee, wanna come out and play?"

"Who's that?" Aaron demanded. The voice had a sinister ring to it, as if the man had been watching B horror movies.

Renee stood frozen in place. Her body trembled. Aaron slipped his arms around her and kissed the top of her honey hair. "Is it Benny?"

She nodded.

*The one who beat her senseless when she was a child, Lord.*

The phone rang. Aaron answered it. "Hello."

"The boyfriend, I presume?"

"Leave her alone, Benny. It's over. Go back home," Aaron demanded.

A wicked laugh pierced the phone. "She's told you who I am. Well, watch your back. I'm watching yours." The phone went dead.

Aaron slammed the phone down.

"Come on, you're getting out of here. It's not safe."

Aaron star sixty-nined the call, but it came back as an untraceable number. "We're going to the police station, and you're filling out a restraining order. This guy won't hurt you again, Renee. I promise. Renee?"

She stood in place, not moving, as if she were in a trance.

"Renee?"

Slowly she turned her head and looked at him. "I need to run."

"No, you're staying with me. You're not running anywhere."

"No, I mean I physically need to run. It reduces the stress. It's my defense mechanism."

"Oh. Can you run after we pack your bags and report this creep to the police?" He grinned.

She smiled. "Yes, but I'll need to run tonight."

"I'll run with you, unless you want to do laps with me in the pool?"

She shook her head. "Nope, I need to run. It helps."

"All right, you can run. But first, let's run into your bedroom and grab some clothes and get away from this guy. We'll order some new locks, a new phone number, and get you secure. But for now, you're staying with me."

"Aaron, stop and think for a minute. I can't stay with you. Your place isn't safe for me either. It's like you said, he's probably already found out where I work, where I run, everything about me. The best thing is for us to stick with the plan of my staying at your parents'—at least for tonight."

He hated that she was right. "All right, but first we pack, agreed?"

"Agreed."

Her cell phone rang. She went to answer it. Aaron took it from her hands. "Hello?"

"Yeah, she's right here, hold on."

He cupped the phone. "It's someone named Jean."

"Jean?"

"Yeah, she says you know her from church."

He watched her mentally calculate whether she knew the woman or not. "Oh." She grabbed the phone. "Hi, Jean." After a brief pause, she said simply, "Fine."

*Fine, my foot. She's got a lunatic running around after her, and she says she's fine.* He stuffed some clothing in a gym bag. He opened her underwear drawer, grabbed a fistful, and plopped it in the bag. He didn't care to look. If he didn't pull out the right stuff, she could buy more. Everyone always needs new underwear, he reasoned.

"No, you know what," he heard her say into the receiver, "I don't think I can make it to the Thanksgiving service after all."

Another brief pause. "Yeah, I know, but something's come up."

*Again, the author of understatements.* Not that he'd want the entire world to know his business either. But two minutes ago she was a zombie, now she was acting like she didn't have a care in the world. *She probably runs in the sun with no hat.* Down here the sun could scramble your brains. That had to be it. No one could turn their emotions on and off that quickly, could they? He certainly couldn't. In fact, he was beginning to work up to a full steam. He needed to calm down before he lost his powers of reasoning.

"Thanks, Jean, I really appreciate it. Adam's really excited. I appreciate your help on that too." Renee looked at Aaron mischievously. "Nope, can't talk right now. He's standing beside me."

She chuckled. "Absolutely. Talk to you later."

Her duffel bag oozed with clothing that dangled from the opening. He stuffed it in and pretended he wasn't curious about Renee's Thanksgiving plans.

# fourteen

"Aaron, sit down and let me explain." Renee held her hands together to keep him from seeing her shaking. "Something you said made perfect sense, but I didn't see it until I was talking with Jean."

He sat down on the edge of her bed. He held the duffel bag between his legs. "What could I possibly have said that would make you want to stay in this unsafe place?"

"It's not unsafe. Okay, tonight it is. But tomorrow I'm coming back." She came beside him and sat down. "Aaron, you said that I needed to trust the Lord. Well, I do. I can't be running from Benny the rest of my life. I'll file a restraining order, but I'm not thirteen, and I've learned some self-defense techniques over the years. I'm going to fight him, Aaron. I have to. Don't you see? It's now or never."

He rubbed the back of his neck and worked the stress out of it.

"Adam and I have gone to a lot of trouble to put together something special," she continued, "and I'm not going to take that away from him."

Aaron let out an exasperated breath. "I suppose you're right. But I don't like it. I want additional protection here."

"Like what? I've got a superintendent who now knows not to let anyone in. I've got a security system in the apartment I can put on "stay," and if someone opens the door, the alarm will go off. I can sleep with the panic button next to me, just in case. Seriously, if we look at this logically, he can only come at me via the elevator. I don't think Benny will walk up seven flights of stairs."

"Okay, but tonight you're staying with me."

"No, tonight I'll stay with your parents," she corrected.

"Then I'll stay there too."

"Aaron," she chided, raising her voice.

"Oh, all right. I'll go home, but Adam stays with my parents."

"Agreed. Now, why don't we call Detective Diaz and see about applying for that restraining order."

Aaron shook his head.

"What?"

"You. One minute you're falling apart, the next you're the rock of Gibraltar."

"Oh. The psychologist said that shock impacts me that way. After the initial shock, I come back swinging."

"Well, keep your bat handy." He grinned.

Playfully she swatted him on the shoulder. "Thanks for being here for me, Aaron. You don't know how much that means to me."

❧

Two hours later Renee found herself at Charles and Gladys Chapin's house. Detective Diaz was skeptical of Renee's claims until he pulled up Benny Gamaldi's file, and she was able to give him details of the dates of his arrest and the court case against him. With the taped phone message and the testimony from Aaron of Benny's phone call, they were able to put in a petition for a restraining order against the man. The judge would have to get an order to unseal her records and verify that this man was guilty of the crimes against her, since his court records only read that he'd beaten a minor.

Her running shoes and clothes on, Renee was ready for a good workout. Aaron insisted on coming with her. She didn't mind the company, but she needed to run hard. He wouldn't be able to keep pace with her. He was in good shape, but he wasn't a runner. They went to the moonlit beach where she could run for awhile and still be well within Aaron's view if he should need to rest. And she knew he'd need to rest.

To warm up, she started with her stretching. "Do you do this every day?" he asked.

"Yup." She bent down and placed her palms on the ground

without bending her legs.

"Ouch, that looks painful," Aaron whined. "You sure you don't want to go to my place and take a few laps in the pool?"

"Chicken?"

"Bock, ba, ba, bock." Aaron imitated the bird with some feet scratching and head bopping along with the clucking.

"Come on, Chicken, I'll run the first lap slow. Hey, what's a good chicken name? I can't call you Chicken all night."

"How about Fred?"

She started a slow jog to the water's edge. The tide was low, providing lots of room for a flat footing. "Fred?"

"Yeah, it's short for Alfredo."

"Whatever happened to Frederick?"

"That, my dear, would be from my father's side, my English side."

"I see, so today you're Alfredo the Spanish chicken?"

"You have to admit, Chicken Alfredo sounds much nicer," he huffed.

Renee laughed. "Any chance we can get some this late at night?" She kept an even pace for him to follow.

"Possibly, but it's more likely we can get your favorite Italian food."

"Pizza," they said in unison.

After a fifteen-minute run south on the beach, she turned and headed north. "Okay, Fred, it's time to beat feet." She poured on the steam. Every step slammed into the sand below her as she pushed herself into a hard, brisk run. She heard him groan but didn't turn back. She went up to the wharf and turned to head south again, having made the distance in seven minutes rather than the fifteen. Aaron wasn't too far behind. She had to give him credit for sticking by her. "Come on, Fred, four more laps to go."

He smiled and watched her pass.

*Lord, I don't deserve this man. He's so special. Help me be worthy of his love and affection.*

The cool evening breeze swept past as her body glistened

with sweat, cleansing itself from the horrors of the day. *Why, after all this time, would Benny be coming after me now, Lord? Shouldn't his temper have waned by now?*

The simple fact was that without her testimony, they wouldn't have nailed him on half the charges they had against him. She'd seen and witnessed too many of his criminal acts. It still amazed her that the police had used a thirteen year old to get to a criminal.

Her breathing deepened as she pushed herself for another lap. Aaron had jumped into the ocean for a quick swim. His lean frame sluiced through the waters as if he were native to the sea.

Her sneakers felt like lead as their weight increased with the water. *Father remove this yoke from me. I can't bear it any longer. Thank You for helping me open up to Aaron. Why have I lived in shame for so long? I was a kid, fighting for my life.* Tears streamed down her face. *Please, remove Benny from my life completely. I don't want to be looking over my shoulder for years to come.*

Aaron swam toward shore. "Hey there, Beautiful, wanna come for a swim?"

Renee removed her sneakers and dove in. "No," she said, sputtering water, "but I wouldn't mind spending some time with you."

Aaron wiggled his dark eyebrows and captured her in his arms. "So, what's this secret you have going with Adam?"

"I'll never tell." She winked, then dove farther into the waves. "Race you to the end of the pier," she challenged.

❧

Aaron worked the kinks out of his neck as he tossed and turned in bed. He and Renee had decided not to talk about Benny and his threats. She'd agreed to stay at his parents' for a couple days until the security changes were incorporated at her apartment. The fact that someone was out there watching, waiting for the right moment to strike, kept him on edge. No matter how logical it was for Renee to stay in her apartment, he couldn't rest. He needed to protect her. The nightmares of Hannah dying in the accident had changed. In the driver's seat, he found Renee, beaten and dying. How could he explain his fear to her? And did he really trust God, as he'd been asking her to do, if he worked so hard to protect her, to overprotect her? Thoughts of sleeping in his car outside her apartment made the only sense for protecting his sanity. Of course, that wasn't fair to Adam, so what could he do?

*Trust the Lord.*

The simple phrase required so much. The irony was that Renee saw him as a pillar of strength with his faith. Only he knew how weak he really was.

He turned to his side and punched the pillow. "Protect her, God. Please don't take her away."

Today was Thanksgiving, a day to celebrate all that God had done for them. To Aaron it had always represented the beginning of Christmas celebrations. Adam and Renee had something up their sleeves for the day. He'd tried to snoop but hadn't found a clue. She was masterful at keeping secrets.

He groaned. If he heard from one more federal agent or police officer that she was not to be trusted, he wasn't too sure he'd be able to keep from exploding. Oddly enough, Diaz had become her strongest supporter. Of course, he was the only one who spent real time with her. Everyone else looked at the paperwork.

Aaron leaned over and picked up the ringing phone. "Hello?"

"Hey, Lazy, wanna open the door?"

"Renee?"

"The one and only. Adam and I have a surprise for you, so get out of bed and come into the living room."

Joy blew away his negative thoughts. The woman he loved and his son were waiting on him. "I'll be right out."

He tossed off the covers and dressed in a pair of jeans and a polo shirt. Brushing his hair, he went to the sink and then took care of his teeth. One quick glance in the mirror, and he entered the living room.

"Happy Thanksgiving, Daddy!" Adam ran up to him. Aaron scooped him up and gave him a great big hug. Yes, he had plenty to be thankful for this morning.

"Happy Thanksgiving, Buddy." He glanced to the living room and found a homemade turkey on the coffee table. Renee stood at the edge of the sofa with a precious smile.

"Happy Thanksgiving, Aaron," she whispered.

He put Adam down and wrapped her in his arms. "Happy Thanksgiving, Renee." He kissed her gently on the lips.

Adam tugged on his pant leg. "Daddy, you've got to see this. You can kiss Renee later."

Aaron and Renee chuckled. "Okay, Sport, show me."

"Look here, Daddy. See?" Adam bounced up and down beside the turkey centerpiece that he must have made with Renee.

"We made it." He beamed.

"It's a wonderful job, Son. How'd you make it?"

"With papier-mâché, right, Renee?"

"Right."

"Open it, Daddy," Adam pleaded.

Aaron lifted the colorful head of the slightly lumpy turkey.

"See?"

Aaron peered inside. "It's my letter to God. Renee said we can write God letters and read them later." Adam leaned over to him and whispered, "You're supposed to write what you're thankful for."

"Ah, thanks," Aaron winked.

"Come see this, Daddy!" Adam grasped his hand and led him toward the back patio.

"What's out here?" Aaron asked, turning back to Renee to mouth the words "thank you."

"More surprises."

Yes, he had a lot to be thankful for. *Help me keep it in perspective, Lord.*

❧

Renee finished cleaning up from the day's activities. Not only had Aaron's parents come, but Marie and her four children had also spent the day at the house. The fried turkey had been a smash, but watching Aaron and his father fish it out with the broom handle had been too precious. Thankfully, she'd caught it on videotape. All five children and the remainder of the adults stood behind the screen wall of the pool.

"Hey, Wonderful, thank you for a great day." Aaron came up behind her and kissed the back of her neck.

A moan of pleasure escaped her lips. "You know what I could really use is. . ." His hands kneaded her shoulders. She groaned. "That's it."

Aaron chuckled. "You've worked hard. I can't believe all the food you prepared. It was a glorious Thanksgiving."

"I haven't had one this special since I was a kid." Changing the subject, she added, "Marie looked good."

"Yeah, Manuel took off again. She and the children are always happier when he's gone. I don't understand why she doesn't see it."

"She sees it; she's just afraid. Afraid she'll be single and alone all her life. At least that's what I figured motivated my aunt. She hated being alone." Renee put the dishtowel down on the counter and turned to face Aaron. "I should be going home."

"What's the hurry? Adam's down for the night. It's the first night you and I've had together in a long time. Or at least it seems that way. Stay for a little while."

"All right, but you can tell my boss why I'm late for work in the morning."

Aaron took her hand and led her toward the living room. "I've met your boss; he's a reasonable man."

"Ha," she huffed. "The man's a slave driver. He gives me tons of work and just leaves."

Aaron chuckled. "Must be because he trusts you."

"Hmm, I've heard rumors." They sat down on the sofa together.

"There is one other possible explanation," he whispered.

Renee closed her eyes as the fine hairs on her arms rose to attention.

"He's fallen madly in love with you and wants to keep you all to himself." He traced her lips with the tip of his finger.

He pressed his lips to hers. She wrapped her arms around him, pulling him closer. Lost in his love, lost in her own for him, could life get any better than this?

An explosion shook the house.

The room went pitch black.

# fifteen

"What was that?" Renee squeaked out the words.

"Sounds like a transformer blew. Sit here, I'll check."

The idea of staying put in a completely darkened house didn't set well with her take-charge approach to life. Renee worked her way to the kitchen and fumbled around the counter until she found the matches. She recalled seeing some candles in—which drawer? She mentally went over the contents of Aaron's kitchen cabinets. Third drawer down next to the refrigerator. Her eyes now adjusted to the darkness, she could see the long, slender white candles still wrapped in cellophane.

A nagging thought crept in from the darkness. What if Benny was behind the power outage? Gooseflesh rose on her arms.

*Stop it,* she reprimanded. *No use making a mountain out of an anthill. The power's gone out, plain and simple.*

*Where's Aaron? Why hasn't he returned?*

She struck the match. A warm glow balled in front of her around the glowing flame. She lit the candle, forgetting to take off the cellophane.

"Oh, for pity's sake," she mumbled and blew out the match. She worked the plastic down the candle and tried the process again. Successfully lighting the candle the second time, she looked for a candleholder. Not finding one, she improvised. Remembering the Cuban coffee cups looked like shot glasses, she retrieved them from the cabinet and melted some wax in the bottom and set a candle in each of the small cups. The three candles lit the area fairly well, but she wouldn't recommend reading in this light.

A thump from the backyard caused her to pause. Was Benny out there? She rushed into Adam's room and made certain the boy was all right. *Lord, why can't they find him and put him away?* She knew it would take more than the restraining order to put Benny away again, but it just didn't seem right that men like Benny could walk the streets, threaten people, and never get caught.

Renee took in a deep breath and calmed herself. No sense getting worked up over nothing, she chided.

*Where is Aaron? Shouldn't he be back by now?*

She left Adam sleeping soundly in his bed and headed toward the front of the house. The front door was open. Cautiously she walked toward it. Her heart raced. Her pulse drummed in her ears. She licked her dry lips and swallowed.

Pausing, she listened. Nothing. Shouldn't she hear something? Anything, a car driving by, something?

"Aaron," she called.

No answer.

She stepped closer to the door.

"Aaron," she called louder.

*Father God, where is he? Please keep him safe,* she pleaded.

A cold sweat rose on her skin. She was nervous, too nervous. She needed to calm down. She placed her bare arms and hands on the cool plastered walls. Reality. She took in a deep breath.

Her hand caught the end of an umbrella Aaron kept by the front door. She wrapped her fingers around it. *A weapon,* she thought. With renewed strength, she forced her steps to the open doorway.

"Aaron," she hollered.

"Over here, Honey." He waved from across the street.

She leaned the umbrella against the interior door casing. He jogged back to her. "Sorry. I was bragging about the deep-fried turkey to Jerry."

*You scared me half to death,* she wanted to say but instead held her tongue and smiled.

"The transformer blew. Jerry said someone saw it blow with a huge fireball. But it burned itself out right away. The power will be down for a few hours. I've got a flashlight in the front hall closet." Aaron went into the darkened house.

Renee shook her head. *I can't believe I was so afraid, Lord.* The shock took hold, and her body started to shake. *Thank goodness it's still dark and Aaron can't see me like this.*

A door opened and various thuds echoed in the empty hall. "Found it," Aaron called out.

"Shh," she warned. "You'll wake Adam."

"Nah, the kid sleeps like a rock." A golden beam of light lit Aaron's chest up to his face. His handsome features calmed her frayed nerves.

"I should probably go," she whispered. "I lit some candles in the kitchen." She rubbed her arms, willing off her earlier tension. It was foolish to live in fear. She knew it, and she refused to be a victim of it. Unfortunately, knowing it in her head was one thing. Acting on it took a bit more persuasion for the body to comprehend.

Perhaps it had been seeing Marie today, knowing her situation, knowing all too well the personal anguish the woman lived through day in and day out. In Marie's eyes, she could see the fear of returning home. *Lord, give her the courage to leave Manuel for her and the children's safety.*

"You're probably right," Aaron answered.

Renee did a mental jerk. *What was he agreeing to? Oh right, my leaving.* "I had a wonderful day, Aaron. Thank you for letting me invade your family."

"Are you kidding?" He came up beside her and wrapped his arms around her. "You made the day, Silly. I can't believe you went to all this trouble. You made it special, Renee, and I appreciate it very much."

"I guess I needed a special holiday," she admitted.

"Honey, since Hannah died, holidays have been less than special. Adam needed this. I needed this. Thank you from the bottom of my heart. I could never repay you for the joy you've given me and my family today." He kissed her lightly on the forehead.

"Good night, Aaron. Thank you."

He followed her out to her car and waved good-bye. *God, help me, I don't want to leave his house. Your will, Lord, not mine,* she prayed as she drove in silence back to her own apartment. Tonight she would face the demons of years past, alone. All alone.

&

Giving in to his insecurities, Aaron called his father and woke him up in the middle of the night. Charles Chapin was a patient man, but Aaron couldn't believe his father actually agreed to come out in response to his two A.M. phone call and for such an irrational reason.

When the older man arrived, Aaron shook his hand. "Thanks, Dad."

"No problem."

Aaron noted the pajamas, slippers, and robe his father had on. He hadn't bothered to change.

"Do you really think her life is in danger?" his father asked.

"Honestly, I don't know what to think. I can't sleep. It's the first night she's alone in her apartment since the break-in. I just know I'll rest more comfortably if I check out her apartment building. See if someone's hanging around."

"But you don't know what he looks like, Son."

"Actually I do. The fellows working with me on the sting pulled up his record and showed me his mug shot."

Charles rubbed the back of his neck. "Be careful."

"Don't worry, I will. I just need to reassure myself that she's okay."

"You could call her," his father suggested. He clicked the light switch. "What's with the lights?"

"Transformer blew shortly after you left. FPL should have it up and running soon."

"Ah, well, I don't plan on staying up all night. If you're going to go check on her, scoot."

"Yes, Sir." Aaron headed toward his van and turned back. "Thanks, Dad."

His father waved him off. Aaron knew the man could have

lectured him about how foolish he was being, but instead he simply came over and took his place watching Adam. It was more than likely Aaron would find him asleep on the sofa when he returned.

The drive to Renee's apartment was peaceful, hardly a car on the road. The cool night air held a relaxing feel to it. He pulled over to the side of the road and waited. In the distance he could hear an occasional car driving on Biscayne Boulevard. A dim light burned in Renee's apartment. Was she still awake? Should he call? Would she be angry that he was outside her apartment building watching out for her?

No, he wouldn't call. *Father, give me peace. I need to know that You're watching over Renee, that she'll be safe. You know I've fallen in love with her. I know I shouldn't have. I should have waited until things with the business were settled. But what can I say, Lord? I want to do what's right. Are You calling us to each other? In so many ways it seems right, but we barely know each other. And yet we connect on such a deep level. Protect her, Lord. Forgive my fears and unbelief. Help me rest in Your sovereign peace.*

Aaron turned the key, put the car in gear, and drove home. There was nothing he could do. She was out of his hands and in the Lord's. That knowledge should make him feel more confident, but it didn't. Hannah's tragic accident flooded back in his memory. Days of asking God "Why?" There were no answers, at least none that satisfied. And now he knew Renee was at risk, and there was still nothing he could do. "A man should be able to do something to protect the ones he loves, Lord."

❧

The following Monday afternoon, Aaron found himself torn between doing what the investigators wanted and being honest with Renee. He didn't want to deceive her, but if the sting was going to work, he had to have her full attention. All afternoon he'd been trying to come up with a plan that wouldn't tell her what was happening but wouldn't deceive her either.

The feds had set up a dummy corporation. Sunny Flo Designs had to put a proposal together for Innovative Trust, a think tank for businesses and social groups.

He had their brochures, corporate vision statement, logo, and target audience. Hopefully, Renee wouldn't ask too many questions. Entering the office, he smiled. "Hi."

"Hi, Honey. How was your meeting?"

"Good. They're interested in having us put together a full multimedia package for them. But first they want to start with a Web page." He handed her the material.

She scrunched up her nose. "Who designed these?"

"They need us," he replied.

"They need an overhaul. This is really bad, Aaron. Did you go over these?"

"Yeah, did all I could to keep a straight face." That was truthful. He glanced at one of the hidden cameras and smiled. He knew they were watching.

Renee continued to work through the haphazard material. "Honey, I'm not about to tell you your business, but do these folks really know what they're doing? I mean, they are setting themselves up as consultants and, and. . ."

"I know, it looks bad, but they're not claiming to be advertising guys, just business advisors."

Renee shook her head. "Don't think I'd want their advice. No offense."

Aaron chuckled. "None taken. Besides, that's what we're here for, to take folks like this and make them shine."

"Hmm, might take a miracle." She scribbled something on the edge of one of the pages. "What about the logo? Is that set in stone?"

"Nope, they want to be completely revamped."

"Okay," she mumbled, continuing to lean over the papers. He loved watching her work. She'd nibble her lower lip ever so slightly when she got a brainstorm.

*There, she's got it*. He grinned. "Knock 'em dead, Renee. Get John to help you with any layouts you need."

"Uh-huh." She didn't look up.

Aaron chuckled under his breath. She'd come up with a great campaign. It was a shame nothing would come of it. Thankfully the government had agreed to pay his normal fees for such a proposal.

"How long do we have?" Renee popped her head up as he sat down behind his desk.

"Two weeks."

She nodded and continued to jot down some notes.

&

*Two weeks! They're asking a lot.* On the other hand, it was more time than most gave for a proposal. But never with this much work. *Innovative Trust. Who thought up that name? Sounds more like a new bank or something.*

"Honey." Aaron's voice nipped at her senses. She paused. Had he called her?

"Renee?"

She glanced over to his desk. "Yes?"

"I said, Adam's waiting for us. I think we better pack it in for the night."

"Oh, sorry. Give me a minute."

He smiled. "I knew you would dive into this one."

"There's no choice. It's a bear of a project. How long has this company existed, and who thought up the name?"

"I think they told me a year and a half."

"Do they have clients?"

"Apparently not enough. That's why they're hiring us."

"Are they? This isn't just a proposal?"

"Well, no—but I figure they'll have to hire us. Who else can do a better job on this?"

"Don't be too sure, Aaron. I'm good, but I'm not a miracle worker. That name—whoever named it that?" she mumbled, grabbing her purse and slipping on her sandals.

*Sandals in December, unbelievable.* Aaron chuckled.

"I'm glad you find this so amusing. Do you know how much time will be involved with this project?"

He sobered and paused. He opened his mouth slightly, then closed it. "I have complete faith in you, Honey."

"Nothing like adding to the pressure," she teased.

"Ah, but I've seen you under pressure. You're a wonder to watch." He wiggled his eyebrows.

*And with those gorgeous chocolate eyes, he could ask me to do anything,* she mused. "Kiss me before I say something logical."

"With pleasure." He captured her and gave her a quick peck on the lips.

*Hmm, it must be later than I thought.* Normally they'd share a warm kiss before picking up Adam, wanting to limit their physical contact in front of the boy.

He led her to the door.

Renee looked up at him as he punched the code on the security pad. "I've been thinking about Christmas and what to get Adam, but I haven't come up with anything. Any ideas?"

"He loves planes, trains, boats, blocks, all sorts of things," Aaron replied.

They stepped onto the sidewalk. Aaron turned around and locked the door.

"I know, but he has a ton of toys. Who bought him all that stuff?"

"Uh, I guess I did, why? Do you think it's too much?" He cupped her elbow and led her to her car.

"I don't know. It seems like a lot, but I can't really judge from my past." He waited while she unlocked the car door. "Are we dropping your car off or mine tonight?"

He looked up at the deep blue sky and grinned. "Mine."

She chuckled. "I'll meet you at your house after I go home and change."

"Okay." He leaned over and kissed her again. This time with a bit more passion. "Bring your bathing suit. I think we'll want to swim later."

She didn't have the heart to tell him she'd left it there Thanksgiving day. He jogged toward his car, looking both ways for oncoming traffic.

Unclasping the roof locks, she lowered the top. Adam loved the top down. Of course, Aaron enjoyed it as well. Not to mention her own particular joy in having the cool wind racing past. She'd have to take a day off and drive through the Keys soon, just for the joy of the ride.

She worked her way through the North Miami traffic and entered the secured garage below her building. Before going upstairs to her apartment, she took the time to put the cover over the collapsed roof. She waved to the super and headed up to the seventh floor in the elevator. Pressing the black button, she watched the doors close.

In her apartment, she kicked off her sandals and stretched her toes. Rolling her shoulders, she strolled into her bedroom and undressed. Seconds later she donned a comfortable pair of khaki shorts and a light cotton blouse. She pulled her hair back in a loose ponytail, did a quick check in the mirror to make certain her makeup was intact, and headed toward the door.

The answering machine's red light caught her attention. She pressed the play button.

"Renee," a voice said, sniffling. "This is Marie, Aaron's sister. I–I don't know why I called really. I guess I just wanted to say hi. We had a good time on Thanksgiving. Thanks."

"That was your last message," the machine droned.

Should she call her? Was she okay? Renee looked up Marie's phone number and punched it in. The annoying busy signal came on. She copied the number and recorded it in her cell phone. She would keep trying. With each passing day, she was enjoying this small wonder of technology more.

Turning her security system back on, she left her apartment and headed toward Aaron's house. Tonight they were going out at dinner to the "peanut place," as Adam liked to call it. She was grateful his all-time favorite restaurant was getting rather old.

She looped her keys around her finger and spun them around. *Father, let me know what to do for Marie,* she prayed.

Sitting behind the wheel of her car, she called Marie again. Still busy. She snapped her phone shut and hooked up the hands-free headset.

She started the engine.

The phone rang.

"Hello," she answered.

"Hello, Renee."

Her body stiffened. She clenched the wheel.

## sixteen

"Dad?" Adam called.

"Yes, Son."

"Is Renee coming with us?"

Aaron looked in the rearview mirror and caught a glimpse of his son wiggling his feet back and forth. "Yup, she's going to meet us at our house."

"Dad?" he sang again.

"Yes, Son." Twenty questions. Would the child ever get beyond this stage? he wondered.

"Can Renee be my new mommy?"

Aaron's mouth went dry. To say he hadn't thought of the prospect would be lying, but they'd only been dating for a couple months. "Ah, I don't know, why?"

" 'Cause I like her, and you kiss her all the time."

*Hmm, he has me there, Lord.* "Well, it takes more than kissing to make a woman your new mommy."

"Why?"

"Because men and women have to know it's right to get married."

"Why?"

"Because God doesn't want us marrying the wrong person."

Adam crossed his arms and knitted his eyebrows.

Aaron took a deep breath. He'd stopped that onslaught of questioning.

"How do you make her a mommy?"

Aaron loosened his tie. "First a man has to ask the woman if she would like to marry him."

"I can do that." He beamed.

*Oh dear.* "No, Adam. I'd have to ask Renee."

"Why?"

*Good grief. How do you explain engagement to a four year old? Father, any wisdom here sure would be appreciated.*
"Because you have to be a man before you can ask a woman."

"I'm a man."

"No, you're my little man. You're not all grown up yet."

"I'm getting bigger."

Aaron chuckled. "Yeah, you are, Buddy, but you still need to be as big as Grandpa or me."

"I like Renee. I want her for my new mommy," he pouted.

"Tell you what, Son. I like Renee too. Why don't we pray and see if she's the one God has picked to be your new mommy?"

"Really? We can ask God?" Renewed excitement filled his dark brown eyes.

"Yeah, we can ask God." The thought wasn't an unhappy prospect. Day by day he'd been falling helplessly in love with her. If only the police would stop hinting that she was involved with the corporate espionage. Logically, he understood their line of reasoning. She had started to work for him shortly before his troubles began, she did have the expertise to set up access to his private files to be shared with others, and she had apparently called in the change of passwords. Something he hadn't asked her about. Partly because he didn't believe she did it, and he wanted her to know that he trusted her.

Detective Diaz made a point of saying he now believed Renee, but the man didn't see how Benny Gamaldi could have played a part in the break-in. He hadn't been released from prison then.

*Who was it?* Aaron rubbed the back of his neck.

His cell phone rang.

"Hello."

"Mr. Chapin?"

"Yes."

"This is Sergeant White from the North Miami Police Department. Are you familiar with a Renee Austin?"

"Yes, she works for me."

"Ah, well, she asked us to notify you."

"What's happened? Spit it out, Man." Aaron's voice rose.

"She's been in an accident. She's at the emergency room at Aventura Hospital."

Aaron clung to the steering wheel. His stomach lurched. "Is she okay?"

"Yes, she'll be fine."

He glanced in the various mirrors and sped up. "Tell her I'm on my way."

"Sure. Mr. Chapin?"

"Yes?"

"She'll need a lawyer. A good one."

❧

"Déjà vu," Renee mumbled. Benny had come at her waving a knife. She'd reacted. Pure instinct had taken over. She'd slammed her car door into him, leaped out of the car, and jump-kicked him in the jaw with her foot. Apparently the self-defense class had paid off.

Silently, Renee prayed, hearing Benny ranting and raving with his claims that she had attacked him. She leaned her head back against the pillow of the emergency-room bed.

"It's her knife," Benny whined.

Her eyes popped open, then she closed them again and tried to remember what the knife looked like. It was possible, even highly likely. After all, he had been in her apartment. He could have stolen it then. *Has he been planning this setup all along?*

*The restraining order,* she thought. Perhaps that would protect her rights against his lies. Memories of the past, her previous arrest, the trial caused her stomach to tighten. "God, no, I can't go through that again," she cried into her pillow.

A sharp pain caused her to groan. "Ugh." She eased out the constrained breath. She hadn't come away from the incident unharmed. The wound to the back of her shoulder now throbbed. The small nicks and cuts to her hands burned.

"How are you?" a young doctor dressed in a white lab coat asked, holding her chart in his hand.

"Alive," she quipped.

"Sit up and let me have a look."

She sat up, and he undid the hospital gown at the base of her neck. A nurse stood silently watching.

"It's not too bad. I'm going to order a CT scan. Are you pregnant?"

"No."

"Any chance of it?"

"No." She knew it was a rational question, but her anger simmered on the surface, wanting to lash out. Thankfully, logic ruled, and she held her tongue.

"The CT scan will tell me if there's damage to the bone and the extent of the tissue damage. Let's check your range of motion."

He put her through a small battery of tests, most of which she could easily perform. Tears hovered on the edge of her lids as the pain increased. The doctor gave his orders to the nurse, who led her down the hallway for the CT scan.

On and on the tests and treatments droned. The officer at the scene now came into her area. "I've called your employer, and he told me to tell you he's on his way. Can you please go over the incident once again?"

Renee nodded her head. She knew the routine. *Lord, help me.* Renee recited her account of the "incident," as he'd termed the traumatic event.

The officer lifted his head and looked at her. "I'm sorry, but—"

"Renee, are you all right?" Aaron rushed into her cubicle with Adam on his hip.

"Renee," Adam squealed and reached out to her.

The officer stepped back and closed his notepad.

"I'll be okay," she said meekly as another man walked into her cubicle, dressed in a business suit and carrying a brief-case. She pulled the covers up to her chin.

"Renee, I've secured Mr. Stein as your attorney," Aaron announced.

She shifted her glance from the stranger to Aaron, back to

the police officer, and then back to Mr. Stein. "What's going on here? Am I being arrested? And how do you know about it before I do?" She glared back at the officer.

❧

Aaron paced the waiting room while Adam sat on a seat and watched the television bolted to the ceiling. He'd never seen Renee this angry before. He couldn't blame her. He'd charged into the hospital with lawyer in tow. Thankfully she hadn't fired the guy on the spot. Why the police officer hadn't informed her and had informed him, he'd probably never know.

He found himself looking at every male coming in and out, wondering if he was Benny Gamaldi. Figuring the man to be a middle-aged Italian, he eliminated half the suspects.

"Daddy?"

"Yes, Adam?"

"I'm hungry. Can we bring Renee home now?"

"Soon, Son. She should be released soon." The question was, would she still be angry with him?

Harvey Stein strolled over to him. "Aaron, Renee asked me to give you a message. She's going to be tied up for awhile and suggested you take Adam home."

"What's the deal, Harvey? She has a restraining order out on this guy."

"True, but he's claiming she attacked him first."

"No way, not Renee," Aaron protested. *If I could just get my hands on this creep,* he thought.

"Look, I think it's highly unlikely too, but let me do my job, okay? Take the kid home. I'll make sure she gets home safe and sound."

Aaron glanced over to Adam. He sat there hugging his knees. The poor little guy was just as concerned as he was for Renee. "All right, but tell her I love her and that Adam and I will be waiting for her call."

"Sure. And Aaron, concerning the other parties who are interested in Renee Austin, let them know I'll give them a full report."

Aaron nodded his head. He'd met Harvey during the investigation being performed by the FBI. Harvey's specialty was white-collar crime. He'd earned Aaron's confidence over the past few months, having given him very helpful and useful information concerning his rights and his company's liabilities if a lawsuit should be pursued. Aaron extended his hand. "Thanks."

"You're welcome. Take the boy home and try to relax. I'll try and smooth things over with Renee."

Aaron stifled a half-hearted chuckle.

"Can we say good-bye to Renee?" Adam asked.

Aaron looked toward Harvey, who nodded. "Sure, Buddy."

Adam jumped up and ran down the hall. Aaron tried to catch up. Somehow yelling in a hospital emergency room seemed inappropriate. He found Adam on Renee's bed and in her arms.

"Call me," Aaron pleaded. She glanced up at him in the doorway. He wanted to go to her, but her eyes warned him to stay back.

"I love you, Renee." Adam hugged her again.

She winced with pain.

Aaron stepped forward. She held up a hand. "Bye, Buddy. I love you too. Don't ever forget that."

*Lord, please, don't take her from us.* Aaron fought his anger and smiled, reaching his hand out for Adam.

Leaving Renee in someone else's care didn't set well with him. But caring for his son was his first priority. Adam didn't need to be in the hospital, and he certainly didn't need to be there if they dragged Renee off to the police station in handcuffs.

His cell phone rang. "Hello?"

"Aaron, help me."

"Marie, where are you? Are you okay? Has Manuel beat you again?" Today would not be the best day for him to confront his brother-in-law. His Christian witness would go down the drain faster than a palm tree could sway in the breeze.

"He's bad, Aaron, real bad. I've never seen him like this before."

"Where are you?"

"At the mall. He won't find me here, and the kids think we're shopping," Marie answered.

"Okay, I'll be there as soon as possible. Meet me in the food court, and I'll buy you and the children dinner."

"All right," she sniffed. "And Aaron, thanks."

"You're welcome." He closed his cell phone. *Lord, help me. I can't be caught up in anger when I address Marie. I need to bring her to a shelter, Lord. A place where she'll get real help. Please prepare her heart that this is the right thing to do.*

"Daddy?"

"Yes, Adam?"

"Is *Tia* Marie hurt like Renee?"

## seventeen

Semi-dressed in street clothes, Renee tried to figure out how to keep her arm bound to her body and manage to put on her blouse. The doctor's treatment was to bind the arm to her body for a couple days to let the torn muscles begin to heal. There had been no damage done to the bones.

"Here ya go, Honey." The thin, middle-aged black nurse named Jessie smiled. She'd been with Renee all evening. In her hand she held up a large T-shirt.

"Thanks." Renee returned the smile.

"Your lawyer said he'll be waiting for you."

Renee nodded. Whoever this Harvey Stein was, she owed Aaron a huge favor. The lawyer pointed out the obvious marks on her body that showed she was in a defensive posture, therefore not the aggressor. Stein had even spoken with Benny and told him if he didn't want to return to prison, he'd best leave town. Renee could have pressed charges. She wanted to, but another part of her wanted to leave the past buried. Duly warned, Benjamin Gamaldi left the hospital knowing that if he so much as passed Renee's line of vision, she would have him arrested.

The police officer informed her that he'd been the one to advise Aaron to get a lawyer because he sensed Benny would press charges against her. His word against her word would have left the officer little choice in the matter, and he would have had to arrest her.

"Thanks again, Jessie," Renee said as the nurse helped her into the T-shirt. She wouldn't be going out for a few days.

"You're welcome. You've got quite a son, looks like his daddy."

She smiled. "He's his daddy's son. We're not married."

"Sorry, my mistake. If you don't mind me saying so, they were pretty worried about you. I swear that man was going to bore a hole right through the floor tiles. He sure can pace."

Renee chuckled and winced from the pain. "Yeah, he gets that way."

He did love her, and she did love him. She shouldn't have been angry with him. It was Benny she was angry with. But he hadn't been handy; Aaron was. She definitely needed to apologize.

Renee stepped out of the area that had been her station for the past three hours. She glanced up at the clock. *Four hours,* she amended.

"Ready?" Harvey Stein asked, his suit coat opened, his tie hanging loosely.

"Yes. Thank you for taking me home."

"Not a problem. Aaron wouldn't have gone home otherwise. Besides, I need to see the area of the crime just in case Mr. Gamaldi has second thoughts and presses charges."

Would she be stuck with this man the rest of her life? *No, I can't think like that,* she resolved.

"Aaron called earlier and asked me to give you a message. He's gone to meet his sister, Marie, and probably won't be home until late."

"Is she all right?" She didn't know what Mr. Stein knew of Marie's situation, but he should be able to answer that question.

"Don't know. He didn't say."

*What happened to Marie?* The message she'd left earlier on the answering machine. . . Renee had forgotten all about Aaron's sister when she met up with Benny. *Benny,* she sighed. *Lord, please keep him out of my life.*

Harvey opened the passenger door to his Ford Explorer. *Aren't lawyers supposed to drive Cadillacs or Mercedes?* "Can you tell me how it is you know Aaron?"

"He's a client."

*A criminal attorney? Something isn't adding up.* "What does Aaron need a criminal attorney for?" *Does he have a past I'm not aware of?*

"A safeguard. He needed to know his rights with the investigation into the corporate espionage. You are aware of that investigation?"

"Yes, but. . .I didn't know he secured an attorney."

"For advice, primarily. And yes, I was aware of you and your past, which is why he asked me to come. He figured I'd be your best defense. Which, if I do say so myself, I was." He grinned.

Renee chuckled. "You were, no question. I saw visions of my arrest. Do you really think Benny's gone for good?"

Harvey Stein looked to the left, to the right, and left again as he exited the parking garage. "That I can't be sure of. I wager he'll hang around for a bit. See if there's a way he might be able to get to you without doing it personally. But after awhile he'll lose interest, and his organization won't give him too much time away. How aware are you of his previous activities before he was arrested?"

"I don't know much. I do know he was a small-time hood for some mob."

"Small-time is right, but in prison he did some favors. You are personal. I hope I convinced him you were just a kid who had paid long enough with no family, your arrest, and your captivity. However, reason doesn't always work with these guys. But the threat of arrest does. And he knows that if he so much as looks at you, I'll have him hauled off faster than he can sneeze. That's a threat he'll take seriously. He's just gotten out and regained his freedom. He won't want to lose that."

"I hope you're right. Tell me, if you can, who besides me are suspects for the espionage?"

❧

The next couple weeks were a blur. Marie was safe in a shelter. Renee was recovering from her wounds, the proposal was intact, and soon Aaron would be addressing the man or woman who was stealing his work.

"Hello," he said, answering the ringing phone.

"Mr. Chapin, this is Detective Diaz. We've located your office equipment."

"Where? When? Do you know who stole it?"

"Hang on." Diaz chuckled. "We've located it, but we haven't caught the man who brought your belongings to the storage area. It appears as if everything is here, but we're leaving it undisturbed and hoping to catch the man who's been coming almost daily."

"How'd you find it, if you don't mind me asking?"

"The manager of the place called in a suspicious activity report. Actually, he was concerned it was a storage center for narcotics."

*A genuine tip. So they do happen in real life, not just in the movies,* Aaron mused.

"Hi, Honey." Renee's gentle voice brought a smile to his face. He certainly loved this woman. *It's been so hard to be close with all the secrets lately.*

He cupped the phone. "Hi. Detective Diaz is on the phone. They found the office equipment."

"You're kidding. Where? Did they catch the thief?" She beamed.

"But that's not the only reason I called you." The detective's words brought Aaron's attention back to the phone.

He held up his index finger, asking Renee to give him a minute. "What else?"

"I have reason to believe we might be looking at your brother-in-law."

"Manuel?"

"Yeah, he fits the description of the man who's been coming around. Do you know why he would steal from you? And why he would hold on to it rather than sell it off?"

So, Manuel had taken to stealing from his family. How much lower could this man go before he saw the truth of his sin? How many more people would have to suffer? "I don't know," Aaron responded, then prayed the police were wrong. What would Marie say if she knew Manuel had been stealing from her own brother? Aaron kneaded the back of his neck.

Renee placed her loving hands on Aaron's shoulders and started to massage them.

He closed his eyes. He could get very used to this.

"We'll keep a lookout on the storage unit," the detective continued, "and I'll notify you as soon as our man turns up. After that I'll need you to come down and identify your belongings."

"No problem." Aaron spoke for a moment longer, then hung up. He turned and captured Renee in his arms. "Thank you. That felt wonderful. How'd your shopping go?"

"Adam and I had a good time. He's quite proud of your presents."

"Oh, should I be doing some snooping?"

"Ha, you'd never find them."

"Oh, is that a challenge?"

"Possibly." She winked.

The question was, did he dare give her the ring for Christmas? Would she accept it? Was it too soon?

"What's the matter?" She brushed his hair from his forehead.

"I have a meeting this afternoon."

"With Innovative Trust, I know. What's the matter?"

"Oh nothing." How could he explain to her what was happening?

She placed her hands upon her hips. "Aaron, when is this going to be over? Just when I think our relationship is deepening, these walls come up. I know it has to do with the investigation, and I'm trying to be patient but. . ."

He kissed her to silence her and whispered in her ear, "Come with me."

He led her to the car. "Honey, trust me, one more day, and I'll tell you everything."

She sighed. "All right, but why couldn't you tell me in the office. . . ?" Her words slowed down as realization filled her. "The place is bugged?"

He nodded.

She jumped away from the car. "How much? I mean did they see us or just hear us?"

"Both," he admitted.

"Great, those Peeping Toms watched when I kissed you. Don't they have any sense of privacy?"

"Honey." He took her by the hand. "They know I trust you. They've watched and seen you do nothing illegal. They've seen when you've come in after hours and worked on the Innovative Trust project."

Red crimson stained her cheeks.

"Honey, I know it's embarrassing, and obviously I've been told about your coming in. But they've come in after you and have looked over all your work. They know you're not the guilty party. Innovative Trust is a phony company. It's a sting I've been planning with the FBI."

"What? I–I spent all that time on, on. . ." She sat down on the curb and buried her face in her hands.

He sat beside her.

An agent approached. "She'll have to remain in my custody."

Renee raised her head. "Who are you?"

"Agent Wyman, Miss. I'm sorry, but your knowledge about the operation. . . I have to stay by you."

"You heard our conversation?" Renee asked and glanced over to Aaron.

"Yes, your car is—"

"I suppose my apartment is also?"

"Only with listening devices."

"Aaron?" she questioned.

"I'm sorry. They insisted. And that's how the emergency services came to your aid so quickly when Benny attacked you."

"You mean I was never in any real danger of being arrested?"

Aaron bowed his head and shook it no. "The local police weren't aware of the situation at the time. So the threat was real from their perspective. Harvey set them straight without exposing the federal agents."

"Aaron, I love you, but I don't know what to do here. I thought you trusted me. I thought—"

"Begging your pardon, Miss Austin, but Mr. Chapin needs to make his appointment if this sting is going to work."

"Renee, believe me, I love you, and I've trusted you all the way."

For some reason his words seemed hollow, trite even. If he really trusted her, why didn't he protect her from this invasion of privacy?

"Agent Wyman, can I go in and get my purse?"

"Yes. Then I'll take you to a secure location."

"Fine." She had little choice in the matter. She loved Aaron too much to stand in the way of this investigation. Wounded pride aside, she'd do what she could to help him.

"Renee, I'm not leaving until I know you believe me," Aaron persisted. "I don't care about the sting. I care about you and me and what the Lord's been building between us. Please tell me you'll let me explain?" He caressed the top of her hand with his thumb. His dark orbs penetrated her senses.

She nodded. She couldn't speak, not and control her tongue.

"Thank you." He kissed the top of her forehead. "I'll be back as soon as possible. They'll take good care of you. I love you." He waved as he ran toward his van.

She stood there frozen for a moment, then turned and headed into the office. The phone rang. Without thinking, she picked it up. "Sunny Flo Designs, Renee speaking."

"Renee?" She could hear Brent's anger.

"Brent, what's the matter?"

"You know what's the matter. I trusted you. I thought you were a Christian. I never in a million years would have thought you would do this to me, Renee. Okay, I admit I ended our relationship badly, but did you have to steal from me?"

"What are you talking about?" Renee collapsed in her chair. "Steal what?"

"Don't give me that sweet innocent talk. I don't buy it, not anymore. How could you do this?"

"Will you stop talking in riddles and tell me what's happened?"

"You know perfectly well what happened. Why would you break in and steal my proposals? You used to be so creative. Did you steal from others when you worked for me?"

"Look, Brent. I'm not sure what you're talking about but—"

Agent Wyman picked up the phone. "Mr. Cinelli, this is Kevin Wyman. I'm an associate of Miss Austin. Could she call you back in a minute?"

"You tell that woman to stay away from me, you hear?"

"Yes, Sir."

*How could Brent think I would ever steal from him. Why? I was his best designer. This doesn't make sense.*

Agent Wyman hung up the phone. Renee heard the electronic hum of a disconnected line. Her life seemed to be singing the same annoying hum.

"Miss Austin, we need to leave. Please come with me."

The bell over the door rang.

"Hey, Renee, what's happening?" John said as he bounced into his seat.

"Not much. I need to go with Mr. Wyman. Can you lock up when you leave?" she asked.

"Sure, where's Aaron?"

"He has a three o'clock with Innovative Trust."

"Ahh, I hope they buy it. We worked hard on that one."

"Yeah." She tried to sound hopeful, but knew she was failing miserably. "I'll see you tomorrow."

"Sure. Don't forget I go home on Saturday. I'll be back after the new year."

"No problem. If I don't see you tomorrow, have a good visit."

John knitted his eyebrows but said nothing. "See ya."

She waved and led Agent Wyman out the door. Thank the Lord he didn't have a trench coat or a field jacket that had FBI written across the back in big bold letters. Instead, he wore a pair of jeans and a light cotton jersey.

"Am I under arrest?" she asked after they crossed the parking lot.

"No, it's more like protective custody. Miss Austin, we need to contact Brent Cinelli. It sounds like he's been experiencing some of what Mr. Chapin's been going through."

*The man was a regular genius.* "Yeah, but I don't think he'd believe me. I hope you catch this creep. Someone's trying to make me look bad, and I want to know why. I don't have any enemies. This doesn't make sense."

"It'll work out. And we know you're not responsible. We've watched you too closely."

"Thanks, I think," she snickered.

⋙

"Mr. Chapin, so glad you could come. We at Innovative Trust believe in doing business differently. Please, join me and Mr. Sutton."

Aaron kept a straight face. Sutton was a young executive type with styled hair, perfectly pressed suit, and a pin-shaped nose that chiseled his face tensed. Was this the man? He'd never seen him before. *Why would he attack my business, Lord? What have I ever done to him?* He playacted along and shrugged his shoulders. "Mr. Yang, I'm sorry, but I thought we had an appointment for me to show you—"

Yang cut him off. "Yes, yes, Mr. Chapin, we do, but Mr. Sutton had an appointment before yours, and I dare say the time has gotten away from me. He was just presenting his proposal. I think you'll be quite impressed with his work."

Sutton's forehead beaded with sweat. He rose to leave. "I should be going."

Agent Yang came up behind him and placed his hand on the man's shoulder. "Please stay, I think you've done a wonderful job on your proposal."

David Sutton cleared his throat. "Thank you, but I wouldn't want to impose on Mr. Chapin's time."

"Nonsense," Aaron grinned. "I'd love to see your work. I'm

sure it's fine, but it can't compare with mine."

Sutton's eyes moved back and forth in rapid fire. He looked to be planning his escape.

"Very well." Sutton coughed.

"I'm sorry, are you coming down with a cold?" Agent Yang asked.

"Something's just caught in my throat." He fumbled over his words.

"Mr. Sutton is with B&J Advertising," Yang offered.

Aaron nodded and rose. "You've obviously impressed Mr. Yang. Perhaps I should let the two of you work out the details of your contract."

A narrow smile slithered up the finely chiseled face of David Sutton.

"Nonsense, Mr. Chapin. I'd like you to see it."

Aaron stopped at the door. "But Mr. Yang, if you like his proposal so much, I'll spare you the time and let you settle things with Mr. Sutton."

"Better luck next time." Sutton stood tall, extended his hand to Aaron, and even sucked in his gut a bit.

Aaron put his hand to the doorknob, then paused. "You know, Mr. Yang, I think I will take you up on your offer. I'd love to see what got you so excited. Guess I'm more curious than I thought."

Sutton's shoulders slumped.

"Excellent decision, Mr. Chapin. Sit, sit." Yang pushed the keys of Sutton's laptop. Aaron glanced over to see the poor man visibly shaking. As the Power Point presentation ended, Yang hit a key to pause the demonstration. "What do you think, Mr. Chapin?"

"I think it's an excellent proposal." Aaron turned to Mr. Sutton from B&J Advertising. "I'm just curious how he stole it from my company."

"You're daft," Sutton squeaked.

"Am I? So if I go over here and click a couple keys, nothing will happen, right?"

Sutton looked over to him, to Yang, then bolted toward the door. Two agents in black field dress with bulletproof vests appeared in the doorway.

"You're under arrest, David Sutton." The agents proceeded to read him his rights.

Aaron took a deep breath and sat back down. "Just answer me one question. Why did you try to implicate Renee?"

"She got me fired from Brentwood Designs. I had a perfectly good career going, then she became Brent Cinelli's lover and, boom, I was out the door like yesterday's trash."

Aaron shook his head.

"You just wait. She's a vicious witch of a woman. And she's got you wrapped around her finger."

With any luck he'd have something wrapped around Renee's finger that had nothing to do with dishonesty and deceit but had everything to do with honesty, love, and grace.

The next few hours were spent going over details of the case with the agents in charge. They informed Aaron how Brent Cinelli's company had been compromised and that David Sutton had also left a trail there implicating Renee. Thankfully, the agents were able to counter Brent's accusations against Renee and show him the evidence against David Sutton. Brent Cinelli provided employee documents and records.

As Aaron worked his way through the city traffic back to his home, he prayed Renee would be there when he arrived. He'd asked the agents to drop her off at his house.

His cell phone rang. He slipped on the headset and pushed the button. "Hello?"

"Daddy, Daddy, I'm scared," Adam cried.

# eighteen

"What do you mean you can't find Adam?" Renee screamed.

"He disappeared," the female officer informed her.

"Disappeared! Little boys don't just disappear. Come on, we're going to find him." Renee ran out the hotel room's sliding glass door and onto the beach. He could be anywhere. She scanned the area.

"You'll have to stay here, Miss Austin," Agent Wyman protested.

She turned back to him. "Am I under arrest?"

"No."

"Then I'm leaving." She ran down to the edge of the shore. "Adam," she hollered. The female officer assigned to Adam came up beside her. "Okay, show me where you lost him."

"I didn't lose him," the officer protested.

"My foot, you didn't. It was your job to protect him, watch him, to make sure no harm came to him. I'd say you blew it."

"I bent down to tie my shoe, and the kid disappeared. He's fine; I'm sure of it." The officer's hands shook.

Renee wasn't going to argue with the woman. She didn't have time. "Adam," she called again.

She went into a full jog. He couldn't have gone too far, she hoped. "Father, keep him safe."

"Adam," she called again. Other parents stood up on the beach, drawn to the commotion. She stopped to talk with a young father playing with his son, who was building a sand castle. "Did you see a small boy, dark hair, Hispanic, come by here?"

"No," the man answered, rising from the sand. "We've been at the water's edge for about thirty minutes. If he passed, I would have seen him."

*Then he must have gone the other way,* she reasoned. "Thanks." She turned and ran harder back in the direction she'd come from. "Adam," she called again.

A swarm of police officers and agents huddled near the patio of the hotel room. "You could help find him," she yelled as she ran by.

After a minute of hard running down the beach, she saw him, at last, standing with another family. "Adam!" Tears filled her eyes.

"Renee!" he shouted and ran toward her.

She scooped him up and hugged him hard. "Thank You, Lord." Tears ran down her cheeks.

"I was so scared. Mr. Mike let me use his phone to call Daddy."

"Thank you." She looked over to middle-aged man with three small girls playing around him.

"You really ought to be more careful," he kindly chastised.

"Someone else was supposed to be watching him. Thank you, I'll take him back to the hotel."

"His father's on his way here," Mr. Mike informed her.

"Granddad, can we play with our new friend?" the oldest of the three girls asked.

"Can I?" Adam wiggled in her arms.

She didn't want to let go. "Sure, Buddy."

"Apparently he wandered off," she murmured, keeping her eyes focused on Adam.

"He said he was chasing a seagull."

Renee nodded. "Thanks for rescuing him."

"No trouble. As you can see, I have three granddaughters of my own. They can move quickly."

A nervous chuckle escaped her throat. "Yeah, they sure can."

"Ms. Austin," the female officer called, approaching them, "Mr. Wyman would like to speak with you."

"Later. I'm waiting here for Mr. Chapin."

The woman opened her mouth to protest, then clamped it shut.

A squeal of brakes turned Renee's head toward the parking lot. Aaron. She smiled and waved. "Adam," she called, "Daddy's here."

He jumped up and ran to his father. *I love those two so much. Could it ever work out for me to be Aaron's wife and Adam's mother?* The real question was, would he ever fully trust her?

❧

Aaron held his son tightly to his chest and shook. *Thank You, Lord. He's all right.* Renee came up beside him, and he pulled her into their embrace. He kissed them both. "Adam, why did you wander off?"

"I'm sorry, Daddy. I was chasing the seagull."

"You're forgiven, but don't do it again."

"I won't. I was scared. Mr. Mike is a nice man."

"Yes, he is." Aaron glanced over to the middle-aged man and smiled. "Let me put you down, Sport." Aaron walked over to "Mr. Mike," as Adam called him, and expressed his thanks once again. How fortunate Adam had been that Mr. Mike was a teacher at a local Christian school and had come to the beach with his granddaughters. Aaron couldn't stop thanking the Lord enough for watching over his son.

Soon the small family made their way to his van. "It's over, Renee," he whispered in her ear. "We caught him."

"Who was it?"

"Do you recall a David Sutton?"

"He used to work at Brentwood Designs. He couldn't produce on our timetable."

"Apparently he's been blaming you for his job loss."

"You mean all of this is because of me?" She stopped at the edge of the parking lot.

"No, it's all because one man, David Sutton, was greedy and too lazy to work on his own. It seems to me that if he'd taken the time he spent breaking into our system and setting you up and applied it to his own job, he might not have felt the need to use you."

Renee shook her head. "But what about the break-in? The robbery?"

"That we don't know about yet. Maybe David hired some-one. We should know soon. Right now, I'm exhausted. Let's go home."

Renee nodded and nibbled her lower lip. Aaron massaged her shoulder. "Later," he mouthed the words. Renee smiled.

"Daddy, are the bad men gone?"

"Yes, Son, all gone."

"Daddy?"

"Yes, Son."

"Can we tell Renee our secret?"

Renee looked over to him. "Nope, she has to wait until Christmas." *Seven more days to Christmas. Can I wait that long?*

"Okay." Adam shifted his gaze up to Renee. "Renee, Daddy has a surprise, just like we do."

"Hmm, should I try to find it?" She ruffled Adam's hair.

"It's wrapped and under the Christmas tree. You can't touch wrapped presents. Daddy said so. It's a rule."

Renee chuckled. "Aaron, I'll meet you at your house. My car is back at the office."

"All right. Should I stop and pick something up for dinner?"

"Hmm, want to grill some steaks?"

"Yeah, I want steak," Adam purred.

"Sounds like a wonderful idea." Aaron held his son's hand. He gave Renee a quick kiss and squeezed her hand before she ran off.

"Come on, Buddy, we've got some steaks to cook."

❧

Since David Sutton's arrest six days before, Renee's life had seemed disjointed. How was it possible to have two men from her past hate her so much that they'd come after her years later? What was it about her that brought out this kind of hatred? Old doubts from when she was a child tried to re-surface. Feelings that she shouldn't be alive if her parents weren't, that she'd caused their accident in some way. At eight years old, it had been hard to realize their deaths weren't her fault.

Renee jumped up and started to run. Running had been her escape for many years. It gave her a chance to pour all her energy into something other than her nightmares. Self-doubt nipped at her senses. She should end her relationship with Aaron before any other demons from her past arrived. He didn't need to suffer because of her. What other skeletons did she have in her closet? There had been no clue David Sutton had blamed her for his job loss. Benny was understandable. Sick, but understandable. David's anger had come from so far out in left field, she still found it hard to believe, except for the memory of the look he'd given her the moment he received the news he was fired. Pure rage and hatred had brewed in his eyes. Looking back now, she could see it. Then, she simply figured he was angry. Who wouldn't be after losing their job?

Ironically, Brent had called to apologize the day after David Sutton's arrest and offered her another job. Renee snickered at the thought and pumped her legs harder. Rounding the corner by the bay, she looked over the tranquil blue water. She slowed down and worked her way over to the water's edge. Stretching out her muscles, her heart rate slowed. "Father, I don't know what to do. Aaron's family has this huge feast planned for the day. I'm supposed to be there. . . ." She turned her wrist and groaned. "A half hour ago. Do I belong there? Should I be there? Am I putting their family at risk? Aaron's had so many losses, especially Hannah being taken away. I just don't want to cause any more trouble for him."

She tossed a stone into the water. "I know, I know, life is filled with heartache and pain but. . ." She picked up another stone and bounced it up and down in her palm. Actually, she noticed, it wasn't a stone but a piece of coral, rough and hard, with delicate pieces of thinner membranes inside. She examined it more closely. To think it was an animal seemed odd. An animal as hard as a rock.

"Life from a rock," she mumbled. Then verses in both the Old and New Testaments came to mind, telling the story of the Israelites being led through the desert for forty years and how a stone produced the life-giving water for the people to drink. She realized how the apostle Paul reminded the Corinthians about this story and pointed out that Jesus is our spiritual rock.

Again she examined the intricate layers of the coral. Every step of her and Aaron's relationship had been bathed in prayer. She smiled and rose to toss the coral into the water. She stopped midway and held it in her palm. This little hunk of coral would be her reminder to look to the Lord—not herself, not her past—and to keep her eyes focused on the spiritual rock, Jesus Christ.

"Renee," Aaron called as he ran toward her.

"Aaron, what are you doing here?"

"Looking for you, Sweetheart. It's not like you to be late. In fact, you're always early."

She smiled. "Perhaps I've adapted to Miami time."

Aaron chuckled. "Never. Your Yankee roots go too deep." He looked at her tenderly. "I've missed you."

"I've missed you too, but we did see each other yesterday."

"Yeah, but that was hours ago. Seriously, I was afraid something had happened to you."

"I'm fine. I should have called. I haven't gotten into the habit of running with my cell phone."

"I'll forgive you this time." He kissed her tenderly on the lips.

She wrapped her arms around him. "Where's Adam?"

"At the house. I was also afraid you wouldn't come today, knowing how full the house would be. Mother is quite disappointed. She was planning on having you help her in the kitchen."

"I'm sorry."

"Don't fret about it. Mother will get over it. I think she just wants to share with you the traditional Cuban Christmas Eve celebrations."

"I am looking forward to it. Although seeing that entire pig roasted. . ." She shook away the thought.

Aaron roared. "You'll get used to it. We do it every Christmas Eve."

"Every year?"

"Uh-huh." He held her close, and they walked back toward her apartment. *Was he thinking permanently?* she wondered.

# nineteen

Aaron looked over the crowd of familiar faces. The house bulged with family. Renee had passed several family members' close inspections. His sister, Marie, sat in a corner talking with *Tia* Ana. Marie looked good, healthy even. She and the children would be moving in with his parents. Her deepest hurt came in learning that Manuel had been hired by David Sutton to steal the office equipment. Currently Manuel sat in jail awaiting his trial. Aaron knew he'd press charges, not because Manuel stole from him, but because once Manuel was in prison, he'd be out of Marie's life for a little while. He prayed it would be enough time for her to grow secure in herself and in God.

Aaron rubbed the back of his neck.

He felt Renee's gentle touch as she started to massage his neck and shoulders. "Aaron," she whispered.

"Hmm," he moaned in silent pleasure.

"Why do you always rub the back of your neck?" Her breath tickled his senses. *Lord, I want to ask her to marry me now.* He glanced at his watch. *Seven more hours.* He sighed.

"When I was a kid, I fell and broke my neck. The doctors fused a couple vertebrae together, and as you can see, I healed nicely. However, as the day wears on or the tension increases, I feel it."

"You broke your neck? And lived?" she blurted out.

Everyone stared in their direction, then started to chuckle, going back to their own conversations.

"Yup. If you look carefully, you can see a thin line from the incision. He could feel her fingertips work through his hair. *Please, let her say yes, Lord,* he pleaded.

"I can't believe this. Why didn't you tell me before?" she asked.

165

He turned and took her into his arms. "Because it never came up. It happened years ago. I don't even think about it. Although having the Jacuzzi has been a blessing." Wanting to turn the conversation from himself, he asked, "So what do you think of the Cuban way of celebrating?"

"Who's celebrating? We're all working." She chuckled.

"True, but tonight comes the feast. Then at midnight we exchange the presents. And of course, by then it will be Christmas Day."

"The pig smells heavenly. I can't believe you build that pit every year."

"Takes up too much of the yard to leave it up year round."

"I'm enjoying myself. It's fascinating. I don't understand most of what people are saying, but there are enough of you who speak English."

"Actually most of us speak English but, as you've noticed, Spanish is a language that shows great expression. It's just natural to speak both." He winked.

"I'm learning."

"Good. You'll do well."

"Daddy." Adam came running up.

"Hey, Buddy, what's up?"

Adam glanced at Renee, then whispered into Aaron's ear, "Did you ask her yet?"

"No," Aaron whispered back. The disappointment on the child's face was obvious. "It will be midnight soon." Adam wiggled out of his embrace and marched over to Renee. Aaron went to stop the child but remembered Renee and the boy had a secret too. *Lord, don't let him spill the beans.*

Adam whispered into Renee's ear. Aaron tried to hear their conversation. *Lord, please,* he prayed again.

Renee giggled. Aaron eased out a pent-up breath.

"Daddy, I'm taking Renee out to see the pig."

"Okay, Buddy." Adam led Renee by the hand out the patio door to the backyard. Children splashed in the pool. Others sat around in the various chairs talking with each other. Soon he'd have a full family again. If she'd accept him.

ها

The succulent smell of roast pork made Renee's stomach gurgle. She shouldn't be hungry. She'd been eating all day—Cuban pastries, croquettes, nuts, cookies. Then there was the taste-testing of everything from the black beans and rice to the plantains. "See, Renee, Grandpa and Uncle Jorge can turn the pig by picking up here and flipping it," Adam informed her. Excitement oozed from the small boy's pores.

She had to admit the technique was quite ingenious. They used regular chain link fence to wedge the split pig, then put poles on both sides for support and easy handling. They said it would take seven hours to cook this pig, which weighed around eighty pounds. The pit was actually above ground and made of concrete blocks that they could easily take down and store for the next time.

Adam soon found one of his cousins to run with. As warm as the family had been to her, Renee still felt out of place. She helped in the kitchen by doing everything that was asked, but she wasn't much use except for chopping and assembling pieces into pots. Not to mention Aaron's kitchen was tiny—a typical Florida kitchen with cupboards on both sides and a narrow walkway between them. For a small family it was sufficient. For this mob. . . Well, it was best not to speak her thoughts. They all worked well with each other.

Renee wandered back into the living room where Aaron sat beside an older woman with a regal posture. She had bone structure similar to Aaron's father, Charles. Aaron's grandmother, Renee recognized from pictures she'd seen earlier. Aaron's glance caught hers, and he gestured for her to come over. He stood up. "Grandmother, this is Renee. Renee, this is my grandmother, Harriet Chapin."

"How do you do, Dear. It's so nice to meet you. Aaron's been telling me so much about you."

"It's nice meeting you too."

She patted the seat next to her. "Please, sit down and visit with me."

Renee sat down, pulling her skirt past her knees.

"Excuse me, ladies, I'm being paged." Aaron squeezed Renee's hand and left.

Harriet Chapin had royal blue eyes and silver gray hair, finely placed into a bun adorned with sparkling red stones. These same stones made up her earrings and necklace.

"That's a beautiful stone," Renee said. "What is it?"

"Red jasper. My late husband, Quinton, God rest his soul, gave them to me years ago for Christmas. He purchased them on a business trip to Africa. They aren't expensive, but I love the red. I've worn them every year for Christmas." She leaned closer. "And whenever Quinton and I had a special anniversary to celebrate."

"They're beautiful."

"Thank you." Harriet leaned a little closer still and took a quick scan of the room. "Adam told me about your surprise gift for Aaron."

"Oh?" *Just how many people has Adam told?* she wondered. She couldn't blame the poor boy. He'd been carrying the secret for weeks. Of course, Charles and Gladys Chapin also knew.

Harriet whispered confidentially, "I think a family album's perfect. I haven't seen it yet, but I know my grandson will love the gift."

Renee's love and respect for this woman grew. She understood Aaron.

"After Christmas you must pay me a visit. I have some more pictures for you to put in the album. I went through our old photo albums and even contacted my sister-in-law to see if she had some photographs. We have Chapin pictures going five generations back. I know it's a gift for Aaron and one day for Adam, but the entire family is going to want a copy of it."

Renee smiled. "It's funny you should say that. I've been thinking of putting it all on the computer."

"That would be wonderful! Of course, us old folks wouldn't mind a paper copy." Harriet sat straight up in her chair. "But we'll have plenty of time to get a copy."

"The pig is done! The pig is done!" Adam cried out from the backyard.

Harriet slowly stood up. "This is part of the tradition. All gather in the backyard and watch them take the pig off the pit." Renee followed Harriet.

Aaron came up from behind, grabbed her wrist, and pressed her forefinger to his lips. She turned and followed while the others went toward the backyard.

"Renee, I only have a couple minutes. It doesn't take long for the family to come back into the house after the pig is removed from the pit."

"What's the matter, Aaron?" She rubbed the top of his hand with the ball of her thumb.

"Nothing's the matter. I just wanted to have a little private time with you."

She grinned. "I like your grandmother."

"She's a sweetheart. But seriously, Renee, I need to speak with you."

She stiffened. "All right."

"No, no, nothing bad. Oh, goodness. . ." He fumbled for the small box he'd placed in his front pocket. *I don't know why I'm so nervous.* He bent down on one knee.

She gasped, placing her hands over her mouth.

"Renee, I love you, and I prepared a wonderfully romantic speech, but for now I just need to know, would you do me the honor of becoming my wife?"

Her eyes glistened from unshed tears.

"I was going to ask you at *misa del gallo,* but I couldn't wait until midnight. And I figured you might not like to be embarrassed in front of my entire family. Please, Renee, I've never felt more certain of God's choice in my life. Will you marry me?"

"Yes!" she burst out.

He stood up and handed the small package to her. "Open it."

Her hands shook as she tore off the wrapping. She paused, holding the blue velvet case in her fingers, then carefully opened the lid. "Oh my. Aaron, it's beautiful."

"I guessed at your size. The jeweler says he can resize it if we need him to. May I?"

She held out her left hand for him. He kissed her ring finger, then carefully slid the ring onto it. Rainbows of color sparkled from the polished diamond.

"It's three bands of gold," Aaron explained. "One band for you and one band for me—both of those are the yellow bands. The third is white gold, and that represents the Holy Spirit. In Ecclesiastes 4:12 the Bible states, 'Though one may be overpowered, two can defend themselves. A cord of three strands is not quickly broken.'

"With all that we've been through over the past couple months," he continued, "I felt this Scripture really applied to us. What do you think?"

Renee found her voice. "I think I love you. I can't believe this. I've wanted it, prayed for it, but I was afraid to believe it was possible."

"Renee, I love you. I want you to be my wife, my helpmate, my friend, and the mother to our children. All of them."

"I want that too. I love you."

"Then kiss me and seal this deal," he crooned.

She leaped into his arms and kissed him soundly on the lips. "Have mercy," he moaned and recaptured her lips once again.

A round of cheers and whistles came from behind them. Slowly they pulled apart, but he held her close.

"Daaad!" Adam dragged out his name. "The pig is done. Didn't you hear me?"

"Yes, Son." Renee and Aaron joined the rest of the family and roared with laughter. "Merry Christmas, Renee. Welcome to my family."

"Merry Christmas, Aaron. I'll enjoy getting to know every one of them."

# A Letter To Our Readers

Dear Reader:

In order that we might better contribute to your reading enjoyment, we would appreciate your taking a few minutes to respond to the following questions. We welcome your comments and read each form and letter we receive. When completed, please return to the following:

Rebecca Germany, Fiction Editor
Heartsong Presents
PO Box 719
Uhrichsville, Ohio 44683

1. Did you enjoy reading *Cords of Love* by Lynn A. Coleman?
   ❏ Very much! I would like to see more books by this author!
   ❏ Moderately. I would have enjoyed it more if

   _____

   _____

   _____

2. Are you a member of **Heartsong Presents**?  ❏ Yes  ❏ No
   If no, where did you purchase this book? _____

   _____

3. How would you rate, on a scale from 1 (poor) to 5 (superior), the cover design? _____

4. On a scale from 1 (poor) to 10 (superior), please rate the following elements.

   ____ Heroine          ____ Plot
   ____ Hero             ____ Inspirational theme
   ____ Setting          ____ Secondary characters

6. How has this book inspired your life?_____
_____
_____

7. What settings would you like to see covered in future **Heartsong Presents** books? _____
_____
_____

8. What are some inspirational themes you would like to see treated in future books? _____
_____
_____

9. Would you be interested in reading other **Heartsong Presents** titles? ❏ Yes ❏ No

10. Please check your age range:
    ❏ Under 18        ❏ 18-24
    ❏ 25-34           ❏ 35-45
    ❏ 46-55           ❏ Over 55

Name _____
Occupation _____
Address _____
City_____ State_____ Zip_____
E-mail _____

# Homespun Christmas

For the good citizens of Hope, Washington, the future appears hopeless—until a small boy's crazy idea for a *Homespun Christmas* begins to turn things around.

Can the Christmas wishes of one small boy ignite the fires of optimism in the citizens of Hope once again?

Contemporary, paperback, 352 pages, 5 ³/₁₆" x 8"

❤ • ❤ • ❤ • ❤ • ❤ • ❤ • ❤ • ❤ • ❤ • ❤ • ❤ • ❤

# Heartsong

## HEARTSONG PRESENTS TITLES AVAILABLE NOW:

# **Presents**

## **Great Inspirational Romance at a Great Price!**

**Heartsong Presents** books are inspirational romances in contemporary and historical settings, designed to give you an enjoyable, spirit-lifting reading experience. You can choose wonderfully written titles from some of today's best authors like Hannah Alexander, Andrea Boeshaar, Yvonne Lehman, Tracie Peterson, and many others.

*When ordering quantities less than twelve, above titles are $3.25 each.*
*Not all titles may be available at time of order.*

# _H_EARTSONG ❤ PRESENTS

# Love Stories
# Are Rated G!

That's for godly, gratifying, and of course, great! If you love a
thrilling love story but don't appreciate the sordidness of some
popular paperback romances, **Heartsong Presents** is for you. In
fact, **Heartsong Presents** is the only inspirational romance book
club featuring love stories where Christian faith is the primary
ingredient in a marriage relationship.

Sign up today to receive your first set of four, never-before-
published Christian romances. Send no money now; you will
receive a bill with the first shipment. You may cancel at any time
without obligation, and if you aren't completely satisfied with any
selection, you may return the books for an immediate refund!

Imagine. . .four new romances every four weeks—two historical, two contemporary—with men and women like you who long
to meet the one God has chosen as the love of their lives. . .all for
the low price of $10.99 postpaid.

To join, simply complete the coupon below and mail to the
address provided. **Heartsong Presents** romances are rated G for
another reason: They'll arrive Godspeed!

# YES! Sign me up for Heart❤ng!

**NEW MEMBERSHIPS WILL BE SHIPPED IMMEDIATELY!**
**Send no money now.** We'll bill you only $10.99 post-
paid with your first shipment of four books. Or for faster
action, call toll free 1-800-847-8270.

NAME _____

ADDRESS _____

CITY _____ STATE _____ ZIP _____

MAIL TO: HEARTSONG PRESENTS, P.O. Box 721, Uhrichsville, Ohio 44683
or visit www.heartsongpresents.com